CONVOY OF FEAR

Other novels in the *Convoy* series

CONVOY OF FEAR

Philip McCutchan

St. Martin's Griffin
New York

CONVOY OF FEAR. Copyright © 1990 by Philip McCutchan. All rights reserved.
Printed in the United States of America. No part of this book may be used
or reproduced in any manner whatsoever without written permission except in
the case of brief quotations embodied in critical articles or reviews. For
information, address St. Martin's Press, 175 Fifth Avenue, New York, N.Y. 10010.

Library of Congress Cataloging-in-Publication Data

McCutchan, Philip.
    Convoy of fear / Philip McCutchan.
        p.   cm.
    ISBN 0-312-16607-9
    1. World War, 1939–1945—Fiction.   2. Great Britain—History,
Naval—20th century—Fiction.   I. Title.
PR6063.A167C655   1990
823'.914—dc20   90-37304
                                                              CIP

First published in Great Britain by George Weidenfeld & Nicolson Limited

First St. Martin's Griffin Edition: August 1997

10 9 8 7 6 5 4 3 2 1

CONVOY OF FEAR

ONE

It was the time of dark now: full dark in the Grand Harbour as Kemp and his staff left the *Wolf Rock* in the motor-boat for HM destroyer *Probity*. An unusually dark night for Malta; cloud had come, brought by a wind from the Levant in the Eastern Mediterranean, an unpleasant, damp wind. Kemp turned in the sternsheets of the motor-boat to wave back at Captain Champney in the *Wolf Rock*, Commodore's ship from home waters until now; and at Jake Horncape in the *Langstone Harbour* that had just about scraped in to Malta with her so desperately needed cargo of foodstuffs for the garrison under siege.

Two crippled ships; and the main body of the eastbound convoy yet to be taken through to Alexandria and then the passage of the Suez Canal for Trincomalee.

'A hell of a long way,' Kemp said suddenly.

'Sir?' This was Sub-Lieutenant Finnegan of the RCNVR, the Commodore's assistant. 'Where to?'

'Trinco, Finnegan. Where else?'

Finnegan grinned in the darkness. 'Sorry, sir.'

'That's all right, Finnegan. I was just thinking aloud, that's all. All those casualties . . . and so far yet to go.'

'Yes, sir.' Casualties there had certainly been, to ships as well as men. One troop transport sunk, plus four armaments carriers, plus a destroyer of the escort. A cruiser disabled but fighting on. One WRNS officer killed by the bomb that had lodged aboard the *Wolf Rock*, another taken to Bighi Hospital

5

in Malta with a broken back and a leg clumsily amputated by the *Wolf Rock*'s doctor, himself now dead. To date, not a happy convoy. As the motor-boat came alongside the destroyer that would carry the Commodore's staff out to sea to overtake the convoy for Kemp to hoist his broad pennant aboard the troopship *Orlando*, Finnegan looked along the decks. The WRNS draft for Trincomalee had been sent across a little earlier, and First Officer Jean Forrest was talking to the destroyer's first lieutenant. The latter, Finnegan saw, was wearing a bloodstained bandage around his head in place of his cap.

Commodore Kemp, as he scrambled aboard *Probity*, was saluted by the first lieutenant.

'Captain's apologies, sir. He's on the bridge.'

'I'd expect him to be – I don't ask for ceremony, Number One. Are we clearing away at once?'

'Yes, sir, just as soon as your party's aboard.'

As Petty Officer Ramm, in the rear and chivvying his guns' crews, came aboard, Kemp heard the ring of the engine-room telegraphs and felt the vibration from aft as the screws began turning. *Probity*, already headed for the exit from the Grand Harbour, went ahead fast. Not a moment too soon: the air raid sirens were starting. As the destroyer, her engines up to full power now, went past the arms of the breakwater, the dive-bombers were heard from the direction of Sicily and soon after this the ack-ack was pumping upwards from the Malta garrison.

Finnegan's thoughts turned to Third Officer Susan Pawle, helpless in Bighi hospital. The Germans had little respect for the Red Cross.

ii

Probity wasted no time: she went ahead at her maximum speed, hastening to rejoin the escort and deliver the Commodore to his new ship. She was untroubled by the dive-bombers, whose current target was Malta itself.

Petty Officer Ramm looked back as Malta began to vanish

astern, and sucked his teeth a little as he reflected on what had been so near and yet so far: Strada Stretta, The Gut as it was known to generations of naval men, the thoroughfare where every other place was a bar – the Royal Oak Bar, the Royal Sovereign, the Victory, the Valiant, the Ramillies – and in between were brothels. The shore-going tastes of the British Navy had kept Malta very nicely in business, kept her afloat since Nelson's day, and Ramm had had cash burning a hole in his pocket.

But there was always another day, or would be if he came through this lot. That day wasn't likely to come at Alex: there, the transports would break off for troop delivery to Montgomery's build-up of an army to be thrown against Rommel and the Afrika Corps, so far victorious in the desert war. What remained of the convoy would head on east with a reduced escort, and once again the Commodore and his staff would transfer, this time to one of the armaments carriers bound through to Trincomalee in Ceylon. Ramm's time would come there, in Trinco. Kemp would surely be given a while in Trinco before returning to the UK with another convoy. You had to relax some time or other.

Ramm stayed on deck, watching out ahead for the convoy. He was joined after a while by Yeoman of Signals Lambert, also of the Commodore's staff.

'All right, Yeo?'

'S'pose so.'

Ramm looked sideways. 'What's that mean, eh?'

'No bloody mail,' Lambert said.

'In Malta? Didn't expect any, did you? We were the first ship to get in out of the UK since –'

'Yes, I know. I didn't really *expect*. Stands to reason.'

'Hope springs eternal. Hope, otherwise known as a bloody miracle.'

'That's about it.'

Ramm understood; mail from home was the lifeblood of the matlow overseas, and in wartime it wasn't delivered by air. Ramm and Lambert had nattered during the course of the convoy, and Ramm knew that the yeoman was worried about his old woman – there'd been some sort of *contretemps* about a

7

french letter found in Lambert's pocket the night before his last leave was up, and they'd parted on uneasy terms, Lambert's explanation having not stood up to scrutiny. He'd been dead anxious ever since the convoy had left the Clyde: he hadn't wanted to fall out over a misapprehension. He'd found it hard to convince his missus that all prudent seamen carried precautions, just in case, even if they never made use of them. As for Ramm, he had his own problems and preferred not to get any mail from Pompey just in case it held a bomb. The barmaid from the Golden Fleece could be a bomb as lethal to his home life as anything Hitler could drop.

Lambert said suddenly, 'Arse-end Charlie, see 'im?'

Ramm stared ahead. They were starting to approach the convoy. The big, bluff counter of a straggler was just about visible through the darkness and the overcast brought by the Levanter. On her port quarter one of the escorting destroyers was acting as sheepdog. *Probity* went ahead, closed the rear end of the columns, weaving dangerously through the escorts. Ramm went about his business, mustering his gunnery rates for the transfer to the *Orlando*, which would be a tricky manoeuvre carried out with both ships under way, though at reduced speed. Fifteen minutes later, with the Commodore's staff standing by on the destroyer's fo'c'sle, *Probity's* captain made up towards the great, camouflaged side of the liner, like a cliff face rearing above, his engines moving at slow and his bows nudging towards the ladder that had been lowered from the starboard gunport door, the place that in peacetime had been the first-class passenger entry up the gangway from the dockside at Tilbury.

iii

With Finnegan behind him, clutching sheaves of paper in a buff-coloured cardboard folder, John Mason Kemp was taken up a number of ladders and stairways into the deck officers' accommodation and up further to the bridge. *Orlando* had been a liner of the Orient Steam Navigation Company on the same run to Australia as Kemp's own peacetime company, the

Mediterranean–Australia Line. Kemp, now Commodore RNR, and Robert Bracewell, Master of the *Orlando*, had met often in Sydney where both companies had turned their ships round for home, Bracewell being then staff captain in the *Otranto*.

Captain Bracewell welcomed Kemp with a salute. 'Welcome aboard, Commodore.' He grinned. 'I'm honoured – but at the same time I hope you'll not make me into a prime target!'

'No more than you are already, Captain. The enemy's not impressed by the added attractions of the Commodore, I fancy.'

'Well, I hope you're right. Bad luck about the *Wolf Rock*.'

'Just one of many. The losses –'

'Yes, I know. They've been really bad this run. I had many old friends aboard the *Orduna*.'

'Of course. I'm deeply sorry.'

Bracewell gave him a shrewd but covert look. Kemp looked a lot older than when last they met in Sydney, older in fact than he'd looked at the convoy conference on the Clyde. He was taking things hard. Bracewell said, 'Yes, well, don't ever blame yourself. It wasn't any fault of yours, Commodore.' He changed the subject, asking briskly if Kemp had any special orders.

Kemp answered as he'd answered Captain Champney aboard the *Wolf Rock*: 'Your ship, Captain. I'm a virtual passenger. But I'd appreciate the freedom of your bridge –'

'Of course –'

'The same for my assistant.' Kemp introduced Finnegan. 'RCNVR – American by nationality. Entered Canada and fixed himself a war job before the Americans came in.'

Bracewell said, 'Good show,' and shook hands with Finnegan.

'Likewise for my yeoman and his two signalmen working in watches. Then there's my gunnery PO – Petty Officer Ramm. You'll have your own DEMS ratings, of course, to man your armament. I hope they'll not think of Ramm as an intruder.'

'They'll make him welcome enough, Commodore.' Bracewell paused. 'There's something else, isn't there?' There was a twinkle in his eye. 'The WRNS draft?'

'Yes. A damn nuisance in a ship crammed with troops. But

9

First Officer Forrest is a good hand, has them well under control, and we've got rid of a problem in Malta, a pregnant Wren rating,' Kemp said in reference to Wren Smith discovered to be pregnant on passage without having first taken the precaution of a wedding ring. East of Suez where passions at sea ran high, a promiscuous Wren Smith would have been a menace . . . Kemp left it and made an enquiry about the OC Troops.

Bracewell said, 'The brigadier's playing bridge. He asked to be excused coming up to meet you.'

'I see.' Kemp raised his eyebrows but went on, 'Well – never mind. It's not immediately important. Where am I to be accommodated, Captain?'

'My spare cabin. I'll send someone down with you –'

'Don't bother!' Kemp grinned. 'I know the geography of your Orient ships, Bracewell.' The Orient Line and the Mediterranean–Australia Line had always had their vessels built by Vickers-Armstrong at the Barrow-in-Furness yard, and mostly they had been laid down to the same pattern of construction. Kemp took his leave of the Captain and with Finnegan went below to the Master's spare cabin, a comfortable apartment with two square ports, now with deadlights obscuring them, looking out over the fore part of the ship from immediately below the bridge. After taking delivery of the file of documents, Kemp dismissed his assistant.

'Off you go, Finnegan. Have a word with Miss Forrest, make sure the WRNS draft is settled in, will you?'

'Aye, aye, sir.' Finnegan tore off his American-style salute, capless, something that irritated Kemp normally but tonight he was too weary to react. The last few days were catching up with him and he needed a good long sleep. In the morning he would go through his written report for the Admiralty which, on landing at Alexandria, would be put aboard the first ship for the United Kingdom. Before pulling off his outer clothing Kemp reflected on the OC Troops: Brigadier Pumphrey-Hatton, commanding the infantry brigade embarked aboard the *Orlando*, was said to be a difficult character. The Flag Officer in Charge at Greenock on the Clyde had sketched him verbally for Kemp's benefit after the sailing conference. A

10

short, spare man, late of the Duke of Cornwall's Light Infantry in which regiment you had to be short and spare to endure its 140 to the minute marching step. So far, so good; but there was more to Pumphrey-Hatton than that. He was irascible, pompous, self-opinionated and a snob. Kemp, whilst disdaining ceremony in general terms, felt his nose slightly disjointed that the OC Troops would not interrupt a bridge session in order to welcome the Convoy Commodore aboard.

iv

'All right, Miss Forrest?'

Jean Forrest sighed; she, like Kemp, was tired. 'Yes, I think so. The girls have been comfortably accommodated . . . so far as the exigencies of war permit, that is. Two ten-berth cabins.'

'Well away from the troops?' Finnegan asked.

'Yes. But not all that far from *your* ratings.' Jean Forrest frowned. 'I wish your Petty Officer Ramm had been left in Malta.'

'No reason to do that, ma'am —'

'No, I know. It was just a wish. That man's a lecher, and currently a frustrated one.'

'There'll be nightwatchmen, I guess. I've seen one lurking. If you like, I'll have a word with whoever runs the nightwatchmen's duty roster. Chief Steward, I guess.'

'No, don't do that, Mr Finnegan.' She laid a hand on the sub-lieutenant's sleeve. 'I don't want to make too much of it, and you could tread on the toes of the ship's officers, the Staff Captain probably, and that wouldn't do.'

'Just as you say, ma'am. But give me the tip if you're worried and I'll have a word with the Commodore.'

v

Petty Officer Ramm had made his number with the PO in charge of the DEMS ratings, the men who manned the troopship's four 6-inch guns and the various close-range

11

weapons. Petty Officer Perryman had the non-substantive rate of gunner's mate, the same as Ramm. Perryman, however, had qualified in his rate at the Chatham gunnery school which in Ramm's opinion couldn't hold a birthday-cake candle to Whale Island at Pompey, which had been Ramm's spiritual home. Maybe Chatham was the reason why Perryman hadn't been drafted to a warship of the fleet instead of a troop transport carrying obsolete guns that would likely enough blow up when fired; but Ramm wouldn't go too far along those lines, with his own job in mind. You didn't denigrate your own cloth. Perryman's presence in a capacity below his proper rate was no doubt due to personal decrepitude: Perryman looked well over 50 and at his last gasp, sallow faced, shaky hands, belched a lot which he said was due to indigestion.

'All them alarms. Disturbs proper meals, like, you know what I mean.'

'Can't say as I've noticed.'

PO Perryman belched again. 'Pardon,' he said.

'Granted. When I was at Whale Island,' Ramm began, determined to make an important point early on, 'the parade gunner's mate, 'e 'ad indigestion. Or thought 'e did. Turned out to be ulcers.'

'Name?'

'Eh?'

''Oo was 'e?'

'Poulter.'

'Cor! I knew Poulter. I was gunner's mate aboard the old *Benbow* when bloody Poulter was an OD and cack-'anded with it.' Perryman paused, scratched his head and released a cloud of dandruff onto his jacket. 'Course, they always was a cack'anded lot at Whaley, if you don't mind me saying so.'

Ramm, reflecting that Perryman had just given a fair clue as to his age, kept his mouth shut. Chatham ratings were a scaly bunch to anyone from Pompey or Devonport, so bug-ridden that they were known as Chatty Chats, but it wouldn't do to say so. Being older, Perryman was his senior, a disturbing thought in itself which meant that he would have to step down if Perryman pushed it, and he'd seemed like doing so.

Maybe he, Ramm, could sort it out with the Commodore; if he couldn't, he'd have to surrender his party to PO Perryman for so long as they remained in the ship, but that would be only as far as Alex. Till then, he would have to suffer. Disengaging himself from Perryman, who'd looked set for a long yarn about peacetime commissions, PO Ramm went out into the alleyway and all but bumped into a squat figure moving along like one of Monty's tanks. This was Rose Hardisty, Petty Officer Wren and now, since the two third officers were no longer with them, Miss Forrest's right-hand man, or woman if you didn't look too close. Ramm gave a snigger at his own thoughts.

'You should watch where you're going, PO Ramm.' Miss Hardisty dusted down her uniform.

Old bag, Ramm thought. He said, 'Sorry. You was in the way, that's what.' He added, 'Going to bed the girls down, are you?'

'Check their accommodation, yes.'

Ramm sniggered again. 'And check what else, eh?'

'I don't like insinuations, PO Ramm. Kindly don't make them about my girls.' Miss Hardisty strode away along the corridor, past the cabin doorways to either side. Ramm followed along behind, with no precise idea where he was going; he was totally unfamiliar with the lay-out of great liners with all their decks and corridors and cross-corridors and staircases and ladders, lounges, smoking rooms, bars and restaurants. Ahead of him he saw Miss Hardisty stop and bang on one of the cabin doors. She went inside; Ramm followed on and lingered by the door. This must be the wrennery, he assumed. As he lingered a large figure appeared from a cross-passage, a tall man, ramrod straight, white haired, wearing a dark blue tunic fastened at the neck.

This man halted in front of Ramm. Going up and down on the balls of his feet – like a copper Ramm thought – he said, 'Out of bounds, PO. No male personnel allowed. Right?'

Ramm asked in a surly tone, 'And who might you be, may I ask?'

'Yes, you may ask. Allow me to introduce myself. Name of Parkinson. Nightwatchman.'

Ramm blustered. 'Don't reckon I go much on being spoken to by a nightwatchman.'

'Late Colour Sergeant, Royal Marines. Eastney Barracks. Any complaints about me, address them to the Staff Captain.' Ex-Colour Sergeant Parkinson moved on, hands behind his back. He could almost have been carrying a pace-stick beneath the left arm. Ramm made himself scarce, muttering to himself as he went. Parkinson, moving in the opposite direction, was fixing Ramm's face in his mind. Nasty-looking little bugger, he was thinking, had bed eyes and a hungry aspect. Parkinson took his duties seriously. What the ship's officers got up to was their own business and men would be men; the female peacetime passengers could mostly look after themselves if they wanted to. Often enough they didn't, and that, too, was their own business. But the young girls who composed the WRNS were different in Parkinson's eyes. Obeying their country's call, they were modest and maidenly, young ladies mostly, and they had to be protected when far from home, like little chicks torn from the mother hen. Parkinson felt himself to be personally responsible to the Master and the Convoy Commodore that they were not interfered with or insulted. The Royal Marines had never shirked their duty yet.

Ex-Colour Sergeant Parkinson went into his nightwatchman's cubby-hole at the end of the Wrens' alleyway and brought out a photograph from a drawer. It was a depiction of the parade-ground at Eastney Barracks, with himself saluting the Colonel at an inspection. There was a mirror in the cubbyhole; using it, Parkinson saluted his own image. The salute, he decided, was still as smart as in the photograph.

vi

Kemp slept like the dead and was woken abruptly by the whine of the voice-pipe from the bridge and, simultaneously, the sound of the action alarm. Getting out of bed he looked at the clock on the bulkhead: 0234. Having turned in half dressed, he had only to pull on his duffel-coat and shoes and grab for his steel helmet. He was on the bridge within 60 seconds, just in time to find the sky lit like day and a cruiser of the escort burning furiously.

TWO

'Aircraft, sir,' Finnegan said.

'So I see.' In the red glare from the cruiser, the *Belize*, Kemp could see the dive-bombers coming down on the convoy. As ever, the response of the aircraft-carriers had been swift: the Seafires were in the air and attacking. As Kemp watched, two of the Germans spiralled down, pouring flame and smoke, to plummet into the sea. They hit the water astern of the *Nelson* wearing the Admiral's flag. Everything was firing, all the ack-ack from the escort and the merchant ships; the sky was full of bursting shrapnel. From monkey's island above the *Orlando*'s wheelhouse and chart room, the close range weapons blazed away at the Stukas as they came close. The sea's surface was pock-marked with bombs that had missed their targets. Kemp ducked as a stream of machine-gun fire bit into the troopship's bridge and boat deck. As he did so he saw from the corner of his eye a man in military uniform coming up the starboard ladder to the bridge. Short and spare with a bristling moustache: the oc Troops.

Blood was coming down from monkey's island. Brigadier Pumphrey-Hatton moved clear as some spattered his uniform. He approached the Captain with a curiously jerky gait and there was some conversation. A few moments later the attack pulled away. It had been short but sharp and the Stukas had barely left when the *Belize* blew up with a deafening roar. Debris was hurled into the air along with bodies whose whirling arms and legs could be seen clearly

16

from *Orlando*'s bridge. Another explosion came: the magazines going up. Clouds of steam poured out. A third explosion racked the cruiser and then she was gone, broken in half, stern and bows both pointing up to the sky for a matter of seconds before she vanished. There would be few if any survivors.

'Bad show,' Pumphrey-Hatton said. 'Damn bad show.' He caught sight of Kemp, anonymous in his duffel-coat and steel helmet. 'You. Who're you?'

Bracewell made the introduction. 'Commodore Kemp, Brigadier Pumphrey-Hatton.'

'Oh, so you're the Convoy Commodore – I see.' Pumphrey-Hatton's tone was brisk, a no-nonsense man. 'Lost one ship and transferred. Hope you're not a jonah!'

Kemp was furious. 'I did not lose my ship, Brigadier. The *Wolf Rock* entered harbour as a result of a lot of courage on the part of her crew –'

'Yes, yes, of course.' There was no apology. 'Well, it's not important now, is it? I'll see you in the morning.' The OC Troops turned away, nodded at the Captain, and went back down the ladder.

Bracewell said, 'Don't take that to heart, Commodore. The man's a stinker.'

'Perhaps. Have you carried the Convoy Commodore before, Captain?'

Bracewell looked surprised. 'No, I haven't –'

'I thought not. I was slow to be called. I like to be on the bridge the moment anything's picked up on the radar or is reported from the escort. I'd be obliged if in future you'd see to that.'

'I will, of course. I'm sorry.'

Bracewell's response had been frigid. There was silence for a moment then Kemp gave a short laugh and laid a hand on the Captain's shoulder, already ashamed that he had allowed his fury with the OC Troops to be vented on the liner's Master. 'That's all right, Bracewell. I should have made it clear from the start. My fault.' He gave himself a shake: he was getting old for his job. 'I'll remain on the bridge, at any rate until you have your reports in.'

The reports came quickly: three of the ship's own ack-ack

17

gunners killed on monkey's island. They would be replaced by men from the Commodore's party. There had been a near miss just aft of amidships and some riveted seams had been sprung alongside the engine-room but the chief engineer had reported no worries and all power was intact throughout the ship. When, as was routine, the troops had doubled to their assembly points to be ready in case of abandonment, a corporal had slipped on some vomit on the lower troop deck and had broken a leg.

That was all.

'Long may it be so,' Kemp said. The *Belize* was much on his mind; as ever, the main convoy had not stopped for survivors, and there could have been a few. But you didn't take chances with so many thousands of troops going to their war destinations. Ten minutes later there was a report of a destroyer closing the Commodore's ship and then a loud-hailer came alive. The destroyer was the *Probity*. She had closed the area of the *Belize* and had lowered nets and jumping-ladders and kept a sharp lookout for anyone alive. She had not stopped engines and she had found no men. It was at best inconclusive but war was war.

ii

When the sun was up Kemp snatched a couple of hours sleep and was then woken by the Captain's steward who asked about breakfast.

'Yes, please,' Kemp said. 'Plenty of it.'

'Fried eggs and bacon, sir, sausages, mushrooms, tomato. Toast and marmalade, coffee. Corn flakes if you wish them, sir.'

'No corn flakes, Macey, but all the rest.'

'Coming up, sir.' From force of long habit Macey flicked a yellow duster over the desk alongside the bunk. On the desk he saw three photographs. One of a pleasant-looking woman still pretty even though she must be over middle age; two of young men in naval uniform. The Commodore's family. Macey had no family and, in wartime, was glad of it. Hostages

18

to fortune, were families, always in line for Hitler's bombs whether they were civilians or in the forces. He went along to his pantry and got on with the Commodore's breakfast.

Kemp lingered for a while over his coffee and a cigarette, then climbed to the bridge. Bracewell was below, the *Orlando's* first officer, the senior watchkeeper, was studying the sky and the horizons through his binoculars.

Kemp said good morning and asked the first officer's name.

'Renshaw, sir.' Name and face were unfamiliar; it was quite a while since Kemp had exchanged ship visits in Sydney. He became aware of Finnegan approaching.

'Morning, Finnegan. Anything to report?'

'Only OC Troops, sir.'

Kemp lifted an eyebrow. Finnegan went on, 'He sent up a message, sir. He'd like to see you in his suite as soon as convenient.'

'He would, would he? What did you tell him, Finnegan?'

'I said you were having breakfast, sir.'

'And then?'

Finnegan grinned. 'He didn't exactly say so, but I reckon I got the idea he thought commodores didn't need to eat.'

'I see.' Kemp turned away, took a walk along the bridge wing and back again. He hated pomposity in anybody and that included himself. But there were times when you had to put somebody in his place. He said, 'Finnegan, I'd like you to take a message in the reverse direction: To Brigadier Pumphrey-Hatton, with my compliments. The Convoy Commodore does not leave the bridge at sea other than at his own discretion. If OC Troops care's to report to the Captain's spare cabin in fifteen minutes' time, I'll be pleased to see him. I don't propose to dance attendance on stuffed shirts.'

'Yes, sir. *All* that message, sir?'

'Use your common sense, Finnegan. Censor at your discretion.'

A knock had come at Jean Forrest's cabin door. PO Wren Hardisty entered.

'If I might have a word, ma'am?'

'Yes, of course. Sit down, Miss Hardisty.' She indicated a chair. Rose Hardisty sat, knees together and skirt pulled well down over them, back straight. Thus she had always been accustomed to sit in her nanny days, when sent for by the mistress to discuss little Master Donald or Miss Rosemary. Now, she gave a cough.

'What is it?' Jean Forrest asked.

'It's the girls, ma'am.'

'Well, it would be, of course. Petty Officer Ramm again, and his language?'

'No, ma'am, no. Though he does *lurk*. It's that they're scared. Not all of them, but some. The bombs, ma'am.'

'Yes, I saw that myself.' First Officer Forrest had mustered with her WRNS ratings at their boat station during the attack, and one or two had been hysterical when the *Belize* had blown up. 'It's inevitable, really. Isn't it?'

'Yes, ma'am. It's what they've been through. On the *Wolf Rock*.' Once again Rose Hardisty was seeing the big bomb that had lodged, unexploded, in the after part of the Commodore's former ship right above the WRNS accommodation in what had been spare cabins in the engineers' alleyway. She couldn't free her mind of the dreadful sight of Third Officer Susan Pawle pinned by her legs beneath the iron girder that had been dislodged and that bomb suspended only inches from her. And the other young lady, head and chest shattered and neck broken. She referred to this now. 'They keep seeing it, ma'am.'

'They've got to stop.'

'Yes, ma'am. Easier said than done, ma'am, if you don't mind my saying so.'

'Of course it is.' Jean Forrest sat forward, a worried look in her eyes. 'Have you any ideas?'

'Well, no, ma'am, I haven't, not really.'

Jean Forrest thought for a moment, shaking hair from her

face. 'What did you do in your nanny days . . . say in a thunderstorm at night . . . when your little horrors were frightened?'

'Oh, ma'am, not little horrors, they were never that. Master Donald, he's a major in The Blues out in Africa.' Miss Hardisty paused, remembering how once little Master Donald, aged two and a bit, had called her a fuckum bloosance and she had been very embarrassed when she'd had to ask cook what fuckum meant. 'Well, they did have their ups and downs, that I don't deny.'

'But what did you *do?*'

Miss Hardisty looked embarrassed. 'Well, ma'am. I used to sing to them sometimes.'

'Lullabies, to get them to sleep, that sort of thing?'

'Yes, ma'am.'

'I see. Not suitable for a Wren draft. All the same, it's something to think about, isn't it?'

'I s'pose so, ma'am.' Miss Hardisty was doubtful. But she had nothing else to offer in its place and Jean Forrest didn't seem to have any ideas either. Miss Hardisty, getting up to go, remarked that she was going to have her hands full, watching the girls all the time. In a ship with so many men, you couldn't be too careful and the girls' parents would expect no less of her. Jean Forrest smiled to herself after the PO had left her cabin. The old girl was still a nanny at heart and in the eyes of old-fashioned nannies their charges never did grow up.

iv

The WRNS draft was on other minds as well, that of the ship's purser among them. Purser Rhys-Jones was a large, bald-headed man approaching retirement; like Rose Hardisty he had old-fashioned views. He knew from long experience what women could be like at sea. So often they threw discretion to the wind. When he had first gone to sea as an assistant purser he had had two very firm rules impressed upon him by his chief: one, there were two 'm's in 'accommodation'; and two, never sleep with a woman when her husband is aboard.

21

Purser Rhys-Jones had observed over the years that this rule was frequently broken by passengers. There was so much leisure, so much drink, so much proximity and so much opportunity for cabin crawling. A wife could be anywhere in the ship and could not be constantly watched. What took place could be achieved remarkably quickly when necessary. Purser Rhys-Jones had developed a sixth sense that told him infallibly who was transgressing and who with. Many secrets were locked away in his mind, which was full of disapproval. Rhys-Jones was not only Welsh, but was also, when at home on leave, a devout man, a pillar of his local chapel. And now he was faced with something different from the normal run of passengers. Twenty or so service-women, all but a couple of them young. Rhys-Jones had run his eye over the draft list that had come aboard with the Commodore. All of them Miss. In the ship's own crew, there were two other women, both nursing sisters. That was all; and they, not being part of the military draft which had its own medical staff, kept aloof from the troop-decks. They were safe enough. But the WRNS draft was of a military nature . . . twenty young girls, among a whole infantry brigade. Once East of Suez . . . that was when trouble always started. Purser Rhys-Jones, along with the Captain, the Staff Captain, OC Troops and the Commodore, was in possession of certain knowledge not shared with anyone else aboard other than the senior second officer responsible for navigation and the chief engineer responsible, among other things, for the oil fuel bunkers.

Whilst perusing the stewards' overtime sheets with his deputy purser and Mr Bliss, the chief steward, Rhys-Jones found his mind straying constantly to the WRNS; and when the other two left his office, he climbed to the deck officers' accommodation for a word with the Staff Captain.

Staff Captain Main was drinking a gin with Mr Stouter, chief engineer. Rhys-Jones accepted a lemon squash, with ice, and stated his anxieties.

Main laughed. 'You're an old woman, Rhys-Jones. Let 'em look after themselves, it's not your worry. Not like passengers.'

'They need protection. I'd wish it for my own daughters, after all, I have to think of the position *they*'d be in –'

22

'They're not in the forces, are they? Your daughters?'

'No, they are not,' Rhys-Jones said. His twin daughters Ruth and Megan were doing war work in Barry in Glamorgan, close to home and although almost thirty were closely watched over by their mother. 'But the principle is the same. All those men, with their desires.' His eyes grew large as he thought about it.

Main said, 'Normal desires, I'd say. But they're not rapists. Besides, they have NCOS.' He laughed again. 'So have the girls. Have you seen their PO?'

'Oh, yes, I have. A worthy woman, I'd say. But there is still a danger. Or will be, later on. You know what I mean, Staff Captain.'

Main nodded. He asked, 'What do you want me to do, then?'

Rhys-Jones ticked off items on his fingers. Deck space to be roped off; an internal compartment allocated for the Wrens' sole use; a non-frat order issued to the troops to be strictly observed with punishments for non-compliance; the girls forbidden to make any use of the troop-decks or of alleyways and ladders elsewhere in the ship liable to be used by the soldiers.

'I don't see,' Main said wearily, 'why you didn't bring all this up before.'

Rhys-Jones pursed his lips. 'I have had thoughts since then,' he said. Main lifted an eyebrow but said only that he would think about deck space so long as any barriers were immediately removable in case of emergencies, and he would have a word with the army's orderly room about warnings to the troops. When the purser had left the cabin, Chief Engineer Stouter remarked that Rhys-Jones was basically a dirty old man.

'Chapel stalwarts,' he said. 'Whisky bottles under the pew. Funny goings-on with the choir girls.'

v

At the appointed time a knock had come at Kemp's cabin door

23

and a young army officer appeared, looking very smart and wooden. 'Yes?' Kemp said.

'Orderly Officer to oc Troops, sir. Captain Archer.' The orderly officer was pushed aside and Brigadier Pumphrey-Hatton entered with his jerky walk.

'Move yourself, Archer.'

'Sorry, sir.'

Kemp indicated a chair for the brigadier to sit in. Pumphrey-Hatton took it; Captain Archer remained standing. Kemp told him to take the other chair, and himself sat on the edge of his desk, arms folded. He said, 'Good of you to come along, Brigadier.'

'The mountain had to come to Mahomet, apparently.' Pumphrey-Hatton gave a thin smile, more of a grimace. 'There are matters to be discussed. Important matters.' He glanced across at his orderly officer. 'You don't know about this, Archer, and it's time you and some others did in my opinion.'

Kemp started to say something but Pumphrey-Hatton lifted a hand, peremptorily. 'I know what the orders were at Greenock, Commodore. I also know that the timing was left to *my* discretion. Now that Malta's behind us, I consider the time has come.'

'So long as it's clear the decision's yours,' Kemp said heavily. 'I didn't anticipate any disclosures until we were nearer Alex and the disembarkation.'

Pumphrey-Hatton said, 'I command the troops aboard this transport, Commodore, and it's my brigade that's affected. Understood?'

Kemp gave a brief nod. Pumphrey-Hatton was within his rights.

'Good, so that's sorted out. Now, Archer.'

'Sir.'

'What I have to say is brief enough. It's this. As Commodore Kemp knows, the *Orlando* will not disembark her troops at Alexandria –'

'*Not*, sir?' Captain Archer was astonished.

'That is what I said, and kindly don't interrupt me.'

'Sorry, sir.' Archer, Kemp saw, had gone very red in the face.

'My brigade,' oc Troops went on, 'is under orders for Trincomalee. Not Alexandria. That means, of course, that the *Orlando* will sail on through the Suez Canal with the remainder of the convoy. What's left of it, that is,' he added with a cynical look at Kemp. 'What our disposal will be after arrival, I don't know. But I can make assumptions. In my view, the move has to do with the fighting in Burma. It's possible, I suppose, that we may be transported across the Indian Ocean to land in support of the 14th Army, but I don't know and I'm not to be quoted. Understood, Archer?'

'Yes, sir.'

'Good.' oc Troops turned to Kemp. 'What I wish to discuss, Commodore, is this: the reason for the cloak-and-dagger, as you know of course, is that the War Office doesn't want the enemy to get wind of the passage of what will in effect still be a troop convoy, down the Red Sea and across the rest of the way to Ceylon. They have to be left to think the whole troop movement has been for Alexandria. Now, I don't know what you think about that –'

Kemp interrupted. 'I think the War Office is fooling itself. The moment we leave Alex on an easterly course, the word'll go through to Berlin. The whole damn area must be thick with spies.'

Pumphrey-Hatton nodded and said, 'I agree with you. But the War Office has spoken so that's that. None of them is a fighting soldier, of course. Anyway, you're aware of the rest of the orders.'

Kemp was, and considered the whole thing as full of traps as a dog of fleas. *Orlando* was to be made to appear as though she was leaving Alexandria empty. From the moment the approach to the port began, all troops were to be confined below decks and were to remain out of sight through Port Said and the canal. Only after Suez would they be allowed on deck. Their life would be a red-hot hell. Kemp doubted if any of this would fool the enemy intelligence, who would presumably see for themselves that nobody was being disembarked from the ship at Alex. They just might think she had come out from the UK empty but they would be fools if they did.

Pumphrey-Hatton was going on. 'I want your assessment, Commodore.'

25

'It's all bullshit,' Kemp said briefly.

'I refer to the actual passage. The likely dangers. The likelihood of attack, and from what direction. After Suez.'

Kemp blew out his cheeks. 'Not aircraft. Possibly U-boats, in the later stages. And there's always the chance of falling in with a surface raider, a commerce raider.'

'One of the pocket-battleships? *Admiral Scheer*, say?'

Kemp said, 'They stay mostly in the Atlantic. More likely something like the *Kormoran* as was.' *Kormoran* had been sunk in the course of one of Kemp's own convoys, but there were plenty more like her.

'Sizeable guns?'

'Yes, certainly. But I fancy we shall have quite enough gun power aboard the cruisers. Even though *Belize* has gone.'

'Well, we shall see,' Pumphrey-Hatton said. He ruminated for a moment. 'What about those girls that came aboard with you, Commodore?'

'What about them?'

'Infernal nuisance! Women have no place in war, no place aboard a troop transport most certainly – you know what women are. I don't want any complaints about my troops, you know. I call the presence of those girls a provocation. That's another thing I wanted to discuss with you. Dangling their charms –'

'They're all decent young women, Brigadier. The WRNS have a reputation . . . such as I understand the other women's services don't always have.'

Pumphrey-Hatton's face went purple. 'That's a damned offensive remark!'

'So was yours,' Kemp said coolly.

It was not a propitious meeting. Getting to his feet Pumphrey-Hatton turned to Captain Archer and snapishly suggested he would now have a good deal of work to get on with, preparatorily, having the orders ready for the troops to do their vanishing act when Alexandria hove in sight, and he'd better get on with it. Kemp could see that Archer was about to be chased for his life. As the two officers left the cabin, Pumphrey-Hatton said stiffly, 'I shall not forget that you seem unwilling to co-operate, Commodore. I call that a poor show, d'you hear?'

26

Kemp shrugged and let it pass. He could stand his ground with anybody and costive-minded brigadiers didn't impress him greatly. Nevertheless, there were dangers for the future. OC Troops was responsible for his army draft, but Captain Bracewell commanded the ship. As for Kemp himself, as a commodore he ranked with Pumphrey-Hatton; but as a member of the Senior Service he was technically over the soldier: equivalent army officers ranked 'with but after' the Navy. If it came to action and any question of possible abandonment, there could be fireworks. Pumphrey-Hatton would be the argumentative sort. And it was clear he had taken a dislike to Kemp.

Dismissing OC Troops from his mind, Kemp went back to the bridge. He had a private word with Yeoman of Signals Lambert.

'You'll have had no news from home, of course, Lambert.'

'Nossir. No mail at Malta, sir.'

'Quite. Or at Alex, I fancy. It's always a worry – I know that. But I can tell you something for your private ear, Lambert. I had some despatches while we were in Malta, before we left the *Wolf Rock*. Vice-Admiral Malta . . . wireless cypher from the Admiralty.'

'Yes, sir?'

'Up to then, and since we left the Clyde, there had been no air raids on Pompey.'

Lambert gave an audible sigh of relief. Kemp said, 'You can pass that to Petty Officer Ramm, no-one else. All right?'

'Yessir. Thank you, sir.' Ramm would be glad to have the word: his home too was in Pompey. Lambert watched the Commodore's back as Kemp moved away. Kemp was a good bloke; not many would bother, in the middle of heavy responsibilities – wouldn't even bother to remember where a rating's home was, let alone pass on the contents of a cypher which he really oughtn't to have done, though why the lack of air raids should be kept secret in the Med was a mystery beyond Lambert's ken. But everything seemed to be secret in this war, so much so that it had become a joke . . . sealed envelopes marked TO BE BURNED BEFORE BEING READ, that sort of thing. Lambert was much relieved to know that up to

27

yesterday at all events Doris was safe from Hitler; but the unfortunate episode of the french letter still haunted him.

vi

Petty Officer Perryman – as a courtesy, he considered it to be – took Ramm on a conducted tour of the guns, such as they were. Ramm acknowledged that they were a better protection than what the *Wolf Rock* had had, but didn't reckon much beyond that.

'Load of old weary willies. Obsolete back in '17 they were.'

Perryman was nettled. 'So they may be. They can still fire, though.'

Ramm pulled a face. He was irritated by Perryman's constant belching. Funny, how a repeated sound got on your nerves, made you want to lash out, or scream, or something. The close confines of a ship, for instance the cabin he now shared with Perryman . . . it made you wonder what the Black Hole of Calcutta had been like, all those bodies. He straightened from a close examination of the breech-block of one of the 6-inch. There had been a spot of rust, unseen by Perryman. Chatham gunner's mates . . . Ramm sucked at his teeth. Bloody slack, but it wasn't his place to say so. The Navy's hierarchy stood firm. Any RN gunnery officer seeing that rust would have had old Perryman's guts for garters.

Perryman was staring out to starboard, towards Africa, across a sea that had now turned a deep blue. The Levanter had gone, faster than most Levanters that Ramm could remember. There was no land in sight, but Perryman was still staring and a moment later he uttered.

'Bloody North Africa.'

'Eh?'

'Bloody Rommel.'

'Monty says he's going to knock him for six.'

'Hope he does an' all.' Perryman sounded bitter. 'All them pongoes, all that sand, miles an' miles of it, bloody great sand dunes, getting in the tea, up your nose and ears, in the moving parts o' guns and transport!'

28

'Know a lot about it. Bin there?'

'Eh? No, not me. My nipper's there, though. Well, not a nipper now. Sergeant in the RASC. It's a worry.'

'Course it is. And him worrying about you. Doesn't know how close you are, eh?'

'Not all that close.' Perryman turned as a resplendent figure emerged from a door and came onto the after deck. Khaki-drill with knife-edge creases, field service cap on square, Sam Browne gleaming with spit-and-polish as were the brown boots. Moustache and square brown face, piercing eyes. No pips on his shoulders. Petty Officer Ramm recognized a regimental sergeant-major, a warrant officer equivalent to a gunner RN. A man to be respected. The RSM marched along, left-right-left, eyes front, a cane beneath his left arm and held by his left hand with the elbow at an angle that looked as if it had been measured with a set square. The boots banged the deck at the correct infantry pace. Perryman said in Ramm's ear, 'RSM, trooping staff. The pongoes call 'im Bull's Bollocks. Real name's Bill Pollock, see.'

'And God 'elp Rommel,' Ramm said.

The soldier halted in front of the two petty officers. They came to attention. 'Good morning, Petty Officer Perryman.'

'Good morning, Sar'nt-Major.'

"Oo's this?' The eyes pierced Ramm.

Perryman said, 'Petty Officer Ramm, Sar'nt-Major, joined from Malta.'

'Oh, yes. You're in charge o' them WRNS lot.'

'Nothing to do with me,' Ramm said. 'Got their own PO, female.'

'Name?'

'PO Wren Hardisty.'

'Hardisty, Hardisty.' RSM Pollock was staring Ramm up and down so that he felt like a man who'd left his flies unbuttoned. He was aware that he looked somewhat scruffy: often you didn't shave at sea, though RSM Pollock obviously had. Pollock, he knew, wanted nothing so much as to bawl him out, but again the service hierarchy prevailed. Ramm was the Navy's problem, not that of the army. 'Hardisty. Yes, I saw the name. Where is she?'

'Don't know, Sar'nt-Major. Could be anywhere, sorting the girls out.'

'Yes. Well. I'll be having words with her. The Staff Captain's been onto my orderly room. Ship's purser's worried. I'm not. I know my lads. And they know me. There'll be no hanky-panky unless I've gone soft sudden like. Which I 'ave not.'

RSM Pollock turned smartly about and marched the other way. Then back again. Perryman said it was his daily constitutional. Even when the sea was rough, he clocked up a regular mile.

vii

Malta to Alexandria was three days' steaming at convoy speed, allowing for the zig-zag. Mussolini's submarines lurked beneath the blue waters of the Mediterranean. Before arrival at Alexandria the convoy would pass below Crete. From Crete the German air armadas could strike again. The *Orlando* would pass the German convoy route from Crete to Tobruk. The Mediterranean was no peaceful sea, though when the skies were clear Kemp could easily enough imagine himself to be once again on a peacetime bridge, taking a Mediterranean–Australia liner through to Gage Roads off the port of Fremantle in Western Australia, and on round Cape Leeuwin for the Great Australian Bight for passage to Melbourne and Sydney Heads. Days of sunshine and tranquillity mostly, with everything running smoothly under the direction of the Master with no interference from above the sea or below it, no sudden alarms of war. Well-scrubbed decks, luxurious cabins in the first class, all manner of people travelling to and from the southland, enormous menus in the dining saloon to which the passengers had been customarily summoned by bugle, with a dress-for-dinner call sounded half-an-hour earlier. Dinner jackets and evening dresses, beautiful women, important men, the most important of whom were invited to sit at the Captain's table and, however important, often enough proved to be pompous bores with loud voices.

Too much money, too much leisure.

Kemp was visited by a thought that he knew to be a bad one: were those peacetime days really the best? Of course they were; people were not being bombed, killed, burned, drowned. But he did feel that his purpose now was basically a more worthwhile one than the conveyance, largely, of over-indulging wealth to far-off places. He was part of a tremendous effort to free the world from tyranny; part of the whole sea service that wherever a seaman served was directing its efforts to keeping the sea lanes open, keeping Britain supplied with food and armaments, keeping her from starvation and impotence in the face of the worst evil that had struck the world since Attila the Hun. That was surely worthwhile, worth more than carrying bloated, overfed upper crusts – upper in a financial sense at all events – across the world on the backs of stewards living in squalid conditions down in the bowels of the ship, on the backs of firemen and greasers working in a hell of heat in front of the furnaces in the boiler rooms which in the hot weather, especially, were places of sheer torment and often more than that; Kemp could recall much earlier days when the stokehold gang had had to be brought up on deck in the Red Sea, and packed around with ice blocks from the cold store to bring down their tempera-tures. Some had been beyond the point of recovery. And all for around £12 a month, or less.

Bolshie thoughts, and better not indulged in the middle of a war.

THREE

Dr Alan Crampton, the ship's surgeon – single-handed now, since there were no passengers and the army had its own medical staff, doctors and nurses and orderlies of the RAMC – rinsed his hands and wondered what he was going to do for the rest of the day. Morning surgery had just finished and it had been sheer routine: burns among the galley staff, cut fingers, a couple of men of the ship's DEMS gunnery rates suffering from shrapnel wounds sustained in the earlier attacks on the convoy, and the usual assortment of VD cases that were endemic to any ship's surgeon's list.

Crampton was aware of his nursing sister, Mary McCann, watching him. He grinned at her. 'Dull as ditchwater,' he said. 'Worse than peacetime, isn't it?'

'Yes, Doctor.' Mary McCann's pixie face was a shade wicked. 'Less perks, too.'

'Perks my bottom, Mary, it was hard work sometimes. All those old ladies.' Dr Crampton's mind went back in time. The ship's surgeons used to do visits just like any ordinary GP. Cabin visits, ten bob a time in the tourist section, a pound in the first class. Cases of seasickness, mostly, though from time to time there had been heart cases among the more elderly. The old ladies had been the worst, again just as in ordinary medical practice. They liked to be fussed over and they produced all manner of imaginary complaints in order to get the attention of a ship's officer with crimson and gold stripes on his cuffs. They could afford it, of course, and Crampton, when his bills were settled, had pocketed the money with a clear conscience, though at the same time regarding himself as something of a parasite in a medical sense. The sea stagnated a doctor; he lost touch with the medical main stream, became out-of-date unless he bothered to keep up with the literature. There was time for that at sea, and Crampton did do his reading. That didn't lessen the sense of being in a dead-end job. But at 45 it had been too late to change, and the life was comfortable and well-paid, so he made the best of it. As a bachelor he didn't have any home life to miss out on by sailing away to Australia every three months with around ten days leave in between voyages.

Now, taking off his surgery coat and pulling on his white uniform tunic with the badges of rank on the shoulder-straps, he made a suggestion. He made it every day, in fact, at this time.

'My cabin, Mary?'

'Thanks, Doctor.'

Mary McCann from Galway in Southern Ireland was in her mid-thirties, still attractive in her dark, Irish way, still with plenty of fire in the blue eyes; and she had come to like Alan Crampton in the 18 months she had been in the *Orlando*. He was somehow different from most ship's surgeons. They went to Crampton's cabin, its ports overlooking the after end of C deck; Crampton's steward entered at the press of a bellpush. 'Morning, Sister. The usual is it, sir?'

'Please,' Crampton said.

The usual came: a long gin-and-grapefruit for Sister McCann, a plain fruit juice for the doctor. Crampton, un-usually for a ship's surgeon, didn't drink. He had a reason for this: he'd seen the results in those doctors who did.

'Down the hatch,' he said.

'Good health, Doctor.'

'Good health's not my trade. It's the sick wot pays me wages.'

'You have to stay healthy is what I meant.'

'Yes, I know.' Crampton frowned. 'Responsibility . . .'

'H'm?'

He didn't elaborate. He said instead, 'You don't get a lot of

33

illness at sea, do you? Not real illness. Nothing to stretch one's mind.'

'That's true, sure.'

Crampton studied his glass, watching the slight sway of the fruit juice as it rolled gently to the ship's motion. He said, 'You know, I often think . . . all those troops, packed in like sardines along the troop decks. Ship vastly over-crowded by peacetime standards, *any* standards really. Not good for health.'

'They seem to stay pretty fit.'

'Yes, they do. Surprisingly. What I often wonder is what would happen if ever we got an epidemic with troops embarked.'

'No picnic at all,' Mary said. 'But an epidemic, a serious one, is pretty unlikely.'

'Let's hope you're right. Oh, I wouldn't expect anything this trip, there's not far to go anyway. But if ever we had to take troops through the Canal it could be different. Gyppo tummy might be the least of our worries, Mary.'

Dr Crampton had not been one of those who had been told the precise onward orders for the *Orlando*.

ii

'All right for some,' Petty Officer Ramm remarked to the AB who had succeeded Leading Seaman Nelson, killed aboard the *Wolf Rock*, as Number Two of the Commodore's gunnery party. Not an AB any more, in fact; now acting Leading Seaman, Cardew had been temporarily rated up by the Commodore. That rate might be confirmed by his manning port or it might not.

'Come again, PO?'

Ramm jerked his thumb backwards towards the doctor's cabin ports. 'All right for *them*. I looked in like, saw the pisspot jerker serving drinks. Officers, see? Not that I'm one o' them socialists, far from it. But doctors and nurses, angels o' bloody mercy shouldn't be drinking in working hours, not in front o' the 'ands, bloody boat dry an 'all for everyone but ship's officers.' It was scarcely in front of the hands but it wouldn't be tactful to say so, Cardew thought. He let Ramm waffle on.

'Ships' doctors! Pissy-arsed lot, all of 'em. RN doctors are no better neither. S'pose that bloke 'ad to operate – what then, eh? Fingers shaking like a pair o' knickers on a washing line in a sou'westerly gale. Do an appendix, cut a poor matlow's bollocks off like as not. Talking of which.' Ramm sniggered. 'That nursing sister. All goo-goo eyed, just looking at 'im. You can't tell me nurses are born for medical duties only, oh no! Doctors' perks, they are.'

The leading hand, running a rag over the breech of the 6-inch, risked a joke. 'What about POs? I reckon you got first call on that PO Hardisty. I –'

Ramm's glare silenced whatever had been coming next. 'Don't you talk disrespectful o' your betters, *acting* Leading Seaman Cardew.' He reached out and tapped the fouled anchor that had been sewn on the erstwhile AB's sleeve, the badge of his advancement. 'That 'ook can come off as easy as it went on, right?'

'Sorry, PO.'

Ramm went on his way, muttering to himself. Through the port he saw the ship's surgeon and the nursing sister have a refill. It just confirmed what he'd been saying. As he went for'ard, having nothing in particular to do, but looking busy since Kemp or that Finnegan might be watching from the bridge, he heard the sound of singing coming up from below, via one of the mushroom ventilators. He stopped to listen: girls' voices. The little so-and-sos were having a sing-song. Stuff a duck, he thought as the words of *Beneath The Spreading Chestnut Tree* came up clearly, that's not the sort of song matlows would sing when they got together in the shore canteen in Pompey or Scapa! Old Ma Hardisty must be leading that crap. Just the same, Ramm wished he could see them, beating at their breasts as they carried out the motions in time to the words. King George would have a blue fit.

'It's going to create pandemonium!' Captain Archer said distractedly in the orderly room. There had been much panic discussion between himself, the battalion commanders, the Brigade Major, the various adjutants and the regimental sergeant-majors, all of whom had had of necessity to be told of the orders for Trincomalee. It was, the Brigade Major had said, the typical army cock-up only this time more colossal than normal. The brigade was not equipped to make the traumatic shift from expectancy of the Western Desert to far distant Ceylon and then possibly the jungles of Burma. For one thing, there was the question of camouflage jungle uniforms; one of the adjutants remarked with assurance that this and all else would be provided at Trincomalee. He wouldn't believe the War Office was that stupid, sending a brigade into the jungle and the swamps with only khaki-drill shorts to protect legs against leeches and other unpleasantnesses.

Captain Archer was prepared to believe the worst of the high command. He told a story he'd heard from his brother, who was RN. There had been a pre-war officer living at Hamble near Southampton. He had received orders to proceed immediately to Colombo to join HMS *Southampton*, and had been provided with outward transport aboard a P & O liner. When he reached Colombo he found that his orders had become mixed and he should have gone to Southampton to join HMS *Colombo*. Such was service life. That was when Archer had gone on to say, 'It's going to create pandemonium!'

'It will not, sir.' This was RSM Pollock. 'Pandemonium, sir, will not be created in my orderly room. With respect, sir.'

'Glad to hear it, Mr Pollock. To me, it has all the hallmarks of SNAFU.'

'SNAFU it is, sir, I will agree. But we shall cope, sir, SNAFU or not.'

RSM Pollock had a loud voice. It carried. PO Wren Hardisty heard it as she walked past the orderly room. She pondered on an expression she had not heard before. She made an enquiry of one of her girls, later.

The Wren rating looked surprised. 'Not heard it before, PO?'
'No, never.'
'Situation normal, all fucked up, PO.'
Rose Hardisty went scarlet. And the way the girl had come out with it! No shame. It was little Master Donald all over again.

iv

Next day at 1100 rounds were made by Captain Bracewell and the Staff Captain, with OC Troops, the Brigade Major, the three battalion commanders and RSM Pollock as senior warrant officer. The company commanders stood by in their sections, attended by their company sergeant-majors and platoon sergeants. Jean Forrest stood by in the WRSN day room and PO Wren Hardisty in the girls' cabin accommodation.

As Convoy Commodore, Kemp stood aloof from ship's business. He remained on the bridge, pacing the wing with Sub-Lieutenant Finnegan, continually watching the sky and the horizon to the north. Among the escorts the antennae of the radar aerials were turning constantly as the operators aboard the *Nelson*, the aircraft-carriers, the cruisers and destroyers kept alert for the first signs of any strike from Crete.

So far, since Malta, apart from the one sortie earlier, they had been lucky.

'It can't last, Finnegan,' Kemp said.

'Maybe they're satisfied with what they did before Malta, sir.'

Kemp gave a short laugh. 'I doubt it somehow. We're too good a prize.'

'The Heinies do funny things at times, sir.'

'Such as?' Kemp looked sideways.

'Why, Dunkirk. Let the British Army get away –'

'Not without interruption, Finnegan.'

'No . . . but after that. No invasion. Guess Hitler just didn't follow up.'

Kemp said, 'I understand his stars told him not to.'

'Could be the same again, sir.'

Kemp grunted; he never had believed too much in luck. It tended to run out at awkward moments. Currently it was much too peaceful; and by the following evening the convoy would have reached Alexandria. It was always possible the enemy meant to wait until after their arrival, and then mount a massive attack on the base and harbour. Possible but not really likely: once in the harbour, a large number of troops could be got ashore even under attack, and ships were more surely and effectively sunk at sea. On the other hand, if big ships were sunk in the harbour, that harbour's use would be quite severely restricted. Earlier in the war, the battleship *Queen Elizabeth*, which had carried the flag of the pre-war Mediterranean Fleet, had been attacked by frogmen with magnetic mines, and had been holed to such an extent that she had settled on the bottom and become an encumbrance to vital shipping until she had been refloated a long while after.

Meanwhile the sun shone and the sea remained smooth, still like a peacetime passage. When a message came up for Finnegan from Petty Officer Ramm on the after 6-inch, and Finnegan left the bridge, Kemp's thoughts turned homeward to the cottage in Meopham in Kent where Mary his wife was holding the fort under all the difficulties of war. No help in the house, shortages of everything, food strictly rationed while he ate off the fat of the land; the car laid up for the duration and growing whiskers in the garage – there was petrol available in very small quantities if you had a good reason for needing it, but Kemp had refused to trump up reasons when seamen were dying aboard oil tankers out at sea in their endeavours to keep the vital parts of Britain moving and to feed the engines of the armoured columns and the aircraft and the ships themselves. Kemp had seen too many tankers blown up since the war started, had seen too many men gasping and struggling and burning to death in the blazing contents of the oil tanks that spread out when the explosions came.

'What's it about, Petty Officer Ramm?'

Ramm jerked a hand downwards. 'It's that PO Wren, sir, Hardisty. She came up on deck, all hot an' bothered about the OC Troops, sir, dunno why. Then she went below again . . . after asking me to report to you.'

Finnegan said, 'Bugger. Okay, I'll go below. No clues at all?'

'No, sir. Not that I could make out.'

Finnegan turned away, went into the after superstructure near the tavern bar, and down a staircase. As he approached the section of cabins allocated to the WRNS draft, Miss Hardisty bustled up to him.

'Oh, Mr Finnegan!'

Finnegan put a hand on her shoulder; she was very agitated. 'Tell me all,' he said.

'Yes, sir, I will. It's that OC Troops. He was ever so rude to me and I don't think it was called for, I'm not really used to ships of any sort, sir, let alone big liners –'

'Neither is OC Troops, I'll bet. What happened, Miss Hardisty, just tell me.'

'Yes, sir.' She was almost twittering with indignation. 'He went into the girls' cabins. I wasn't expecting that. My girls have never been inspected, not as to their quarters that is, by a *man*. And it wasn't only that brigadier, it was such a lot of them, all those soldiers. All men. Oh, I just didn't know what to say, that I didn't, when that man lifted . . . one of the girls' smalls it was . . . on the end of his cane. He asked what it was. He insisted, and there was I, blushing. Oh, I was so *mortified!*'

Finnegan kept a straight face. 'What did he go on to say, Miss Hardisty?'

'Oh, I don't know that I can . . .' Miss Hardisty's voice trailed away then she stiffened herself to her task. She had always impressed upon her little charges years ago that if you started anything you must, as a bounden duty, finish it. She went on, 'He said, don't just stand there, woman, answer my damn question. Or do I take it you've never seen a pair of knickers before. That was what he said, Mr Finnegan.'

Finnegan nodded. Gravely he said, 'I'm sorry to hear that, Miss Hardisty. I'll report to the Commodore.'

'Oh, I'd be ever so grateful if you would, sir.'

Finnegan went back to the bridge, being overtaken, before he had cleared the lower decks, by the procession of Captain's Rounds. He pressed himself to the bulkhead of the alleyway as the long line of brass went past, with RSM Pollock bringing up the rear like a sheepdog, marching stiffly as if on parade, cap peak pulled well down so that in order to see his next ahead he was forced to hold his neck at a backward angle.

On the bridge eventually, Finnegan made his report.

Kemp said, 'God! Rude, yes. But talk about a storm in a teacup!'

'Right, sir. But I thought I'd warn you. OC Troops will be stirring things up if I'm not mistaken. I kind of read into it – the knickers and that – that the cabins were not exactly prepared for inspection.'

'Finnegan, I'm the Convoy Commodore. Not a housemaid. Or a lady's maid.'

'No, sir. But as the naval authority aboard, OC Troops is going to reckon the girls are yours. If you see what I mean.'

Kemp blew out his cheeks. 'Bombs and brigadiers. Take due warning, Finnegan. If this war goes on long enough, you may even find yourself with a convoy commodore's appointment! By that time I won't be worrying . . . but I wish you the best of luck.' Kemp glanced at the clock on the after bulkhead of the wheelhouse: Captain's Rounds should be about finished; and any moment the army might be storming the bridge, fulminating again about women in war. But in the event rounds were not yet finished when Yeoman of Signals Lambert reported the lamp flashing from the *Nelson*'s flag deck, with a hoist of flags creeping up to the starboard fore yardarm.

'Message, sir. Flag reports submarine contact by *Probity* bearing red three-five, distance eight miles, probably Italians, sir.'

Kemp said, 'Thank you, Yeoman.' He turned to the officer of the watch. 'Mr Renshaw, sound action stations, if you please.'

FOUR

The urgency of the alarm rattlers sounding throughout the ship scattered Captain's Rounds like ninepins. Bracewell ran for the stairways and ladders, making for the bridge. He was followed by Pumphrey-Hatton. RSM Pollock made for the troop-decks, bellowing the rank-and-file to their stations. A mass of men pulling on lifejackets filled the corridors. Night-watchman Parkinson, ex-Colour Sergeant, Royal Marines, off duty and asleep, woke on the instant, pulled on his uniform and pushed through the mob to take up his rock-like stance at the entry to the Wrens' alleyway. Even with the action alarm sounding, or maybe because of it, lust could out before the girls could get to their boat stations. But Parkinson, to his astonishment, was pushed aside by the egress of the girls, led by PO Wren Hardisty, from below. They were, it seemed, right on the ball.

The two naval petty officers, Perryman and Ramm, shoved their way along the boat deck, going in turn to all the guns fore and aft to chase the crews and report ready to the bridge, where Sub-Lieutenant Finnegan would act as gunnery director, or co-ordinator, though Ramm reckoned he could manage very well without. Ramm reckoned subby didn't know a six-inch projy from a fried egg. In the meantime more reports were coming through from the flag and Kemp was conferring with the troopship's Master.

'Your engines, Captain. I'd like all you've got.'

'You shall have it.' Bracewell had already rung down

41

emergency full ahead on the telegraph and the effect was being felt in the increased vibration. By remote control from the bridge, once all personnel not required for duty below had been reported clear, the watertight doors and firescreen doors were shut, thus sealing off the working alleyways below the troop-decks and isolating the individual sections in what had been the passenger accommodation.

The eyes of the convoy were now on their Commodore but for the moment there was nothing else to be done aboard the *Orlando*. Just watch carefully and wait. Hope that each ship would spot the torpedoes' tracks in time, and alter course towards safety. It looked like a big attack; the further reports had indicated no less than six contacts, closing. The destroyers were churning the water, swathes of white foam from their wakes criss-crossing the blue, the bow-waves creaming over their stems as they raced to intercept.

Kemp looked down at the decks; the lifeboats had been swung out in orderly fashion and lowered to the rails of the embarkation deck. The troops were fallen in, lifejackets on now, standing easy with their NCOs walking up and down in front of the ranks. At the after end of the boat deck Kemp saw the WRNS party fallen in under Miss Forrest and the PO Wren. It was a calm scene; the sun still shone, and the lurking enemy was not in sight. But he was not far away. If the lookouts or the bridge personnel failed to see the track, the disturbance below the water, a torpedo could hit at any moment and the scene would alter fast.

ii

Once the system of watertight doors and bulkheads had been activated to seal the various sections of the ship, individual doors would if required be opened again on permission from the bridge so that the fire hoses could be run out from the hydrants. The men, largely stewards, manning those hoses knew that in the event of emergency those doors would again be shut by automatic control, and that they might well find themselves sealed off by them with no hope of escape. It was a similar sort of thing to the shell-handling rooms aboard the big warships, the spaces where the heavy shells and charges were brought up from the magazines to be sent on the hoists to the gun batteries. The men who went down in action to the handling rooms were sealed in after entry, the hatch over the deep, shining shaft being clipped down hard from above with no corresponding clips beneath to enable the hatch to be opened from below. In extremity, the order would come from the bridge to flood the magazines, and with that order the handling rooms would also flood. The trapped ratings would drown, their bodies rising on the seawater to impact against the big steel hatch.

One of the trap situations aboard the *Orlando* lay in the engine spaces, the engine-room itself and the boiler-rooms. Chief Engineer Stouter stood solid on the starting platform, ready for urgent orders from the bridge, white-overalled and carrying in his fist the inevitable bunch of cotton-waste to help keep his hands clean. He exuded a confidence he was far from feeling. He knew his men looked to him and he must never show fear. But he was afraid and had been ever since the war had started. His father, also a ship's engineer, chief of a freighter in the last war, had been trapped in his engine-room when a U-boat had struck in the North Sea, not far off Hull, not far from home. The young Stouter had never known precisely how his father had died, but his mother had heard the story outline from a survivor, the freighter's third mate. The torpedo had hit just abaft the engine-room and plates had been buckled and so had the exit through the air-lock. No-one had come up, no-one above could get to them before the ship went down. Stouter senior had died in the execution of his duty, and young Stouter had had an imagination. Boiler-rooms in those coal-fired days had held a series of red-hot furnaces; and the boiler-room had led off the engine-room. If the furnaces had shattered, the scene would have been a fiery hell.

The images had stuck; but young Stouter had gone to sea because that was what his dad had always wanted for him and he'd felt in duty bound. And, of course, that war was to be the last ever. The war to end all wars.

Stouter's senior second engineer came to the starting platform. 'All correct, sir. Everything bearing an equal strain as they say.'

Stouter nodded. The starting platform canted sharply as the bridge put the helm over. The senior second said, 'I suppose that means something's close.'

'Could be, yes. Or just avoiding another ship. You know what it's like, with the convoy all over the show.' He smiled, tightly, feeling the fear in the pit of his stomach. 'We'll know soon enough.' He looked along at his engines. Turbines were unspectacular objects, with a sort of calm look, not like the old reciprocating engines, say, with their great flailing beams and pistons and suchlike. Calm now, not so noisy as engine-rooms used to be, but all that could change in a second.

The sound-powered telephone from the bridge whined and Stouter answered. 'Chief here.'

It was the Staff Captain. 'Depth-charging's started, Chief. Stand by for bangs.'

'Thanks for the warning,' Stouter said. He hung the phone back on its hook. He had only just done so when the first of the explosions came. It wasn't all that far off, he calculated. The engine-room seemed to ring and shudder, and flakes of cork insulation fell from bulkheads and pipes. Then another, and another.

Through clenched teeth Stouter said, 'Nothing to worry about, Mildmay. Usual pattern, that's all.'

Mildmay, senior second, nodded, ran his tongue over dry lips. He, scared as hell, wondered how Stouter could keep his cool so well. No nerves at all.

iii

Kemp wiped sweat from his face. That earlier full helm movement had indeed been due to Bracewell having to take emergency avoiding action. One of the armaments ships had swung across his bows, veering suddenly to port. Kemp's assessment was that a lookout aboard the vessel had seen, or thought he'd seen, a torpedo trail. If Bracewell hadn't been

44

dead fast, the two ships would have hit and immense damage, even sinking, caused thereby. Bracewell was very competent and alert; but Kemp hated the personal inaction. It was not his place to handle the ship except in certain circumstances but not to be able to do so was sheer frustration to anyone who had held command at sea.

Anyway, there was no torpedo. The destroyers of the escort were doing good work; they had intercepted in good time and the sea was sprouting columns of water as the depth- charges exploded on reaching their settings. Beneath the water, the Italians wouldn't be happy and they might not linger. In fact, they didn't. But they left two of their boats behind: the first victory signal came from Captain (D) in the destroyer flotilla leader and Lambert reported to the Commodore.

'One kill, sir.'

Then the other; in each case debris and oil fuel had come to the surface, a fair indication of broken hulls but not con- clusive. Submarines sometimes blew oil fuel to the surface as a subterfuge and then went deep, lying low beyond the asdics. Not this time: the next signal reported two hulls breaking surface and the crews asking to surrender. One of the destroyers took them off; the others carried on the hunt, and the subsequent depth-charging was more distant. The damaged submarines were sunk by gunfire from the cruisers.

As the order to secure from action stations came down to him, Petty Officer Perryman fell out the guns' crews. In doing so, he had a word with Ramm.

'Thank God for Musso,' he said.

'Eh? How's that, then?'

Perryman winked, and spat over the side. 'They say 'Itler wanted the Med himself. But Musso, 'e insisted on 'is own back yard. Maray nostrum, greasy fat prat.'

'So –?'

'So they've buggered off as usual. 'Itler wouldn't 'ave.' Perryman spat once more, dismissing the Italian Navy. Ramm went below for a fag, feeling sour. Perryman had been chucking his weight around – giving the order to stand down to Ramm's own guns' crews as well as his own. Not right,

45

wasn't that. The sod should have respected Ramm's partial autonomy or whatever. But now he was stuck with him; the new orders had resulted in a surge of buzzes from the galley wireless. The orders were something that could never be kept dark aboard a ship, of course, and now Ramm knew he would be going through to Trincomalee aboard the *Orlando*. With Perryman. He had better be philosophic about a *fait accompli* but he wasn't happy. Aboard the *Wolf Rock*, he'd been king of his own castle, the only gunnery expert aboard.

iv

Pumphrey-Hatton lingered on the bridge for a while after the abortive attack was over. Watching the distant destroyers, he had given a kind of running commentary to everybody's irritation. The action could be seen without verbal assistance, as Lambert had remarked to his number two, Signalman Lacegrove. Pumphrey-Hatton, Lambert said, liked the sound of his own voice and didn't seem to mind displaying his ignorance of sea warfare.

Kemp was wondering if OC Troops was meaning to make a complaint about the WRNS quarters, but no such complaint came. Pumphrey-Hatton ignored Kemp and spoke to Captain Bracewell.

'My men,' he said. 'ETA Alexandria is – what – 1800 hours tomorrow.'

'That's right.'

'I'll have them out of sight a couple of hours before that, then.'

'It's going to be uncomfortable,' Bracewell said. 'Hellish hot below. Longish, too. We'll not leave until the next dawn, and after that it's Port Said and the canal. We'll get fast clearance in Port Said for the canal entry, but it's twelve hours to Suez. And after that we'll have the Arabian coast in sight for quite a while.'

'Time to get used to it,' Pumphrey-Hatton said briskly. 'In the army we're used to discomfort, you know.'

'Discomfort's not unknown at sea, Brigadier.'

'Good God, man!' Pumphrey-Hatton's tone was scornful. He waved an arm around. 'Discomfort! I wouldn't call this bridge or your own quarters uncomfortable. And all the rest of it. Meals served promptly, no shortages, drink available at the touch of a button. Clean linen.' He paused. 'I was in France in the last war. In the trenches as a subaltern to begin with. My battalion was almost wiped out as it happened. But it's the appalling mud I'm thinking about, the cut supply lines, the lack of communication, the general filth of the dugouts.'

'Ships,' Bracewell said, 'can sink.'

'Well, yes –'

'And when they do, all this vanishes in a matter of seconds. It's not comfortable in the water, Brigadier.'

'I didn't say it was.' Pumphrey-Hatton irritably changed the subject. 'To go back to what I was saying. I'd like you to do what you can to relieve the conditions tomorrow. Trim the ventilators, that sort of thing.'

'That will be done, of course. Is there anything else you require?'

oc Troops seemed unaware of the sarcasm. He said, 'Well . . . is there anything you can think of, Captain?'

'I can think of nothing to relieve the sweat and stink of closely-packed troops shut below decks.'

'Nothing?'

'Frequent baths or showers. Salt water will be available. But the bathing space is limited, as you know.'

'I don't call that particularly helpful. We should all pull together, you know.' Pumphrey-Hatton turned away and went down the ladder to the Master's deck. Bracewell walked across to where Kemp was standing.

He asked, 'Did you hear all that, Commodore?'

Kemp grinned. 'I thought he was going to remind you there was a war on!'

'Just as well he didn't. I might have blown a gasket. I'll bet you one thing: oc Troops will be swanning around the decks while his soldiers are shut down below.'

'Dressed as a seaman, to fool the enemy?'

'I don't think he'd lower himself that far.'

Bracewell turned away again as Purser Rhys-Jones was seen

47

to be hovering at the head of the ladder with a sheaf of papers in his hand. Kemp stared across the water towards his charges pushing through under guard of the escort, the *Nelson* and *Rodney* towering like blocks of flats – Queen Anne's Mansions, the Navy called them. The convoy was badly scarred; and there had been so many casualties. Death wasn't very comfortable; yet OC Troops had had a point. The Navy did have a more comfortable war than the army. They lived in relative luxury in the wardrooms of the fleet as the ship's personnel did aboard the ex-liner transports. At sea you carried all your services with you. Stewards were always at hand; there was never, in Kemp's experience, any shortage of cigarettes, to name just one essential of service life, the sustainer of morale, the first resort in moments of crisis, the thing you looked forward to most when you came off watch from the bridge or the guns or the engine-room or wherever. It was just as important to the land forces, but was often missing.

But it hadn't always been like that. Not in the old days of sail that Kemp so well remembered. That was discomfort of a very high degree; and not so far removed from it today were the conditions aboard the smaller escorts, the destroyers, frigates and corvettes that operated across the North Atlantic in all kinds of weather, mostly in the winter months, with their messdecks awash all the way out from Scapa or the Forth or the Clyde or Londonderry, right through to 40 degrees west longitude and back again. Days and nights when there was no hot food because the galley fires were out, days and nights when clothing and bedding were soaked through and there was nowhere except the engine spaces in which to dry out. As a lieutenant RNR in the last war, Kemp had done his destroyer time and he knew what it was like. Pumphrey-Hatton took no account of that.

Kemp looked at his watch and called across to his assistant. 'I'm going below to my cabin, Finnegan.'

'Yes, sir.'

'Call me in accordance with Standing Orders.' This was a routine phrase; Finnegan knew well enough that Kemp would be on the bridge within half-a-minute of being required. He knew something else as well: Kemp was going below to give First Officer Jean Forrest a lunchtime gin. Kemp himself would stick to orange squash at sea. But for the last few days Kemp and Jean Forrest had been on what Finnegan saw to be good terms, and he wondered just what the score was. At the start of the voyage from the Clyde, the old man had seemed frosty towards the boss WRNS officer, had held her at arm's length. Even, once, blasted her off the bridge . . .

v

'Come in,' Kemp said, in answer to the knock on his doorpost. The curtain was across the open door and Jean Forrest pushed it aside as she entered.

'Morning, Miss Forrest.'

'Good morning, Commodore.'

'Sit down . . . what's it to be?'

'Gin-and-lime, thank you.' Jean Forrest sat down. Kemp gestured at his steward, who knew all about the orange squash for the Commodore. Kemp could have poured the drinks himself, but would risk no talk around the ship that he was drinking alone with the First Officer WRNS, the steward set aside for an assignation. That would never do; the Commodore at sea had to be whiter than white. He wondered at his own motives: Jean Forrest had seemed in his view rather too forthcoming when they had first met and he'd seen, or fancied he'd seen, a need to put her in her place. She had come with an introduction; she was a niece of the chairman of the Mediterranean–Australia Line, and Sir Edward had asked him to be friendly. At first she had seemed as though she might flaunt the relationship. In any case Kemp disliked being asked personal favours in a war situation. What Jean Forrest didn't know was that a commander RN employed on intelligence and security duties had boarded the *Wolf Rock* in Malta and had picked up the WRNS officer's name. Jean Forrest was on some sort of security list – her last appointment had been on liaison duties attached to a War Office department evacuated from London to Blenheim Palace at Woodstock near Oxford. The

49

commander had told Kemp in confidence that Intelligence had picked up the fact that there had been a pretty hot affair with a brigadier and Jean had been badly hurt when it had ended. As a result, she had asked for a posting as far away as possible.

The circumstances induced sympathy in Kemp. He was a worldly enough man, and knew the often base behaviour of his own sex; but the knowledge of the affair made him cautious. Jean Forrest, though younger persons might have seen her as a middle-aged spinster – she was 41 – was attractive and she could well be missing sex as such. Kemp had seen from the start that he'd attracted her; so he had stood off. He was a happily married man who had never been unfaithful in almost 25 years of marriage, even though there had been the many temptations in the liners, even though he had spent something like nine months of every year, on average, away from his home comforts. It had been a strain at times, but he had held fast to his principles. He didn't know even now whether or not those principles were going to come under further strain, and in the middle of a war and a convoy at that. But the fact was that he had come to admire Jean Forrest. She had stood up splendidly to the horrors they had come through in the *Wolf Rock*, stood up to death and bombs and had been a tower of strength to the young girls of the WRNS draft. Kemp would no longer be stand-offish.

But he would be formal, he told himself. For now, anyway.

'All well, Miss Forrest?'

She nodded.

'Finnegan reported that OC Troops had a moan.'

'Of no account, Commodore. He upset my PO Wren. That's not a hard thing to do.'

'So we forget it?'

'Yes.'

Kemp twiddled the stem of his glass. He was not wholly at ease, seldom was with women. What did you talk to them about? Kemp was short on small talk. He fell back on Sir Edward and they talked about him, but he didn't last long. Then she asked how he was getting on with Brigadier Pumphrey-Hatton.

50

'So-so.' He wouldn't say more than that; he wouldn't criticize. Commodore and OC Troops had to work together in as much harmony as possible. Besides, brigadiers could be touchy subjects. But it had been Miss Forrest who had raised it; Kemp knew he was seeing things that didn't exist, but that was perhaps part of his caution. You didn't not mention a brigadier just because of the bedroom antics of another brigadier who was in the past. Suddenly, as Jean Forrest smiled at him and shifted in the chair so that he caught the sharp silhouette of her breast against the sun coming through the opened square port, Kemp found he wanted to know more about that past brigadier. A kind of jealousy? He hoped not. And he certainly wouldn't ask any leading questions. Nor was she likely to tell him anything, so his curiosity would have to remain unsatisfied. They talked a little more. As usual, Jean Forrest refused a second gin.

vi

The following evening as the Mediterranean dark began to come down with its usual swiftness, the *Orlando*, dead on her ETA, made in towards the port of Alexandria and, standing clear of the rusted remains of bomb blasted shipping, let go an anchor in the outer anchorage. With a last exchange of signals the heavy ships of Force H and the aircraft-carriers *Victorious* and *Indomitable* turned away to make back for Gibraltar with the *Nelson*. The cruisers and destroyers, with *Glamorgan* wearing the flag of CS 34 – 34th Cruiser Squadron – remained as onward escorts for the convoy through the Suez Canal and across the oceans to Trincomalee. The battleship *Valiant*, coming up from the Cape, would rendezvous at the other end of the Red Sea. The troops aboard *Orlando* were out of sight; the decks were empty of all but the ship's crew. Pumphrey-Hatton was on the bridge, but was not in uniform. He wore sand-coloured slacks and an opened-neck, dark blue shirt, with a red pullover loosely across his shoulders. Camouflage? Kemp wondered.

As the anchor was let go amid a cloud of rust that drifted

51

upwards across the chief officer standing in the eyes of the ship in charge of anchoring, *Orlando's* sister transport made farther in to disembark her troops. The armaments carriers anchored in their positions as signalled by the King's Harbour Master. Bracewell passed the orders for the anchor to be secured with the third shackle on deck; and when the ship had got her cable and was lying idly on the smooth surface he spoke on the sound-powered telephone to the engine-room.

'Finished with engines, Chief. But I'll want you to be on standby while we're in the anchorage.' Then he spoke to the chief officer who had come to the bridge to report.

'Anchor watches, Mr Bruton. The juniors can take the weight and call me when required.'

'Aye, aye, sir. Do you expect attack?'

'Possibly. Alex is within range of Crete.' Bracewell turned to Kemp and Pumphrey-Hatton. 'I think we deserve some relaxation, gentlemen. I suggest a drink in my quarters in half-an-hour's time. Hitler permitting, that is.'

FIVE

When Kemp went along to the Captain's quarters, it turned out to be not just a drink with Bracewell and Pumphrey-Hatton: he found the army there in some force. Not the ship's military staff: they were from the Alexandria base ashore. There was an infantry lieutenant-colonel in desert rig, a staff major, a Movement Control Officer, a captain of military police, and two officers of the RAMC. Each had a glass in his hand and the air was thick with cigarette smoke.

Bracewell made the introductions and then said, 'Trouble, Commodore. Trouble ahead.'

'Rommel?' Kemp suspected yet another change of orders.

'Not Rommel. Over to you, Doctor.'

Kemp found himself confronted with a major of the RAMC. The major was brief. 'Cholera,' he said. 'In Port Said. Come up to epidemic proportions very suddenly. Not nice, to be passing through.'

Kemp said, 'But surely there's always cholera around to some extent?'

'Perhaps, but it's usually brought under control pretty fast. This time it hasn't been. I expect you can see the dangers, Commodore.'

Kemp could. There would be inevitable contact with the shore in Port Said even though no-one from the *Orlando* would actually set foot on the land. There would be the berthing pilot and the canal pilot; there would be the Egyptian port officials with their myriad forms, a feature of life aboard any ship passing through Port Said, war or no war. There would be contact with the lightermen bringing off the stores as indented for by the chief steward – fresh vegetables, fruit, meat and other items. Some contact was unavoidable.

Kemp asked what the real risks were. 'It's not caught from physical contact, is it, Doctor?'

'Not what I expect you mean by physical contact, no. It's water-borne, principally. But –'

Kemp turned to Bracewell. 'Will you be taking water in Port Said?' he asked.

Bracewell shook his head and gave a short laugh. 'Not this time! Our condensers will have to cope. But it'll make for shortages. Washing facilities, for instance.'

Kemp nodded. 'You were about to go on, Doctor. I'm sorry.'

'I was going to say, the bacilli flourish in the intestines and are voided with the faeces –'

'But voiding of faeces . . . that's not going to occur aboard – not from the shore people!'

The doctor laughed. 'I wouldn't let them use the ship's facilities, anyway. But that's not the point I'm making, quite. If it comes aboard, then every precaution will have to be taken to prevent a very, very fast spread. All those troops, and so little space. It could be worse than a dozen bombs.'

'And the actual chances of it coming aboard?'

The doctor shrugged. 'Very hard to say. Any orders for fresh fruit and vegetables should be cancelled, or if the stuff's essential, and of course I agree it is ideally, then it must be washed in Condy's Fluid. Very thoroughly. Of course, I'll be having words with the ship's surgeon and the medical staff embarked with the brigade.'

It turned out that the doctor was in charge of military hygiene in Alexandria. Epidemics were his speciality; he elaborated a little more and made it sound as though the ship was doomed. Kemp asked if the home authorities had been informed, and they had.

Pumphrey-Hatton broke in. 'You're asking if there'll be a change of orders, Commodore. Am I right?'

'Yes, you are.'

'There won't be. My brigade goes where it's ordered. It won't be put off by a damn bacillus. There's chaps waiting for us in – 'Pumphrey-Hatton bit off what he'd been going to say. '– the other side of the canal,' he finished.

He was right, of course. There was a risk, but it had to be accepted like any other risk in war. The troops wouldn't die in swathes like the Egyptians. A ship was a clean entity, and there was a competent medical staff aboard, and if the thing did strike then they would have to pack the untouched troops in even tighter so that space could be cleared for an isolation unit, but that was Bracewell's worry, not Kemp's. Of course, the shortage of fresh water wouldn't help.

The period of relaxation didn't take place; Bracewell and his Staff Captain had much to do. When the visiting army officers went back ashore, Bracewell called a conference of his senior officers including the ship's surgeon, the chief and senior second stewards also being called in.

ii

At dawn, with no response from Whitehall as a result of the cholera report, the *Orlando* weighed anchor and proceeded the short distance to Port Said. Already the troop decks were becoming unpleasant – far from enough fresh air was coming down through the mushroom ventilators. Already water was short, apart from salt water. Only salt water was now available for washing of bodies, the fresh being reserved for drinking purposes. Salt water, with no small basinful of fresh water to wash away the stickiness, left an unwashed feeling behind it. The complaints were many, and questions were asked only to be left unanswered: the word of the epidemic in Port Said was being kept from the men for as long as possible. But during the morning the senior RAMC doctor made a broadcast over the tannoy, speaking of cleanliness and care with the lavatory facilities and so on. This, without mentioning cholera. The brigade had not been east of Suez before and they put the pep-talk down to normal routine for passing through the Middle East, a part of the world not as clean as Britain.

Petty Officer Ramm, however, was an old hand and he read plenty of what he wasn't supposed to into the doctor's talk.

He button-holed Perryman as the ship passed the statue of Ferdinand de Lesseps at the end of the breakwater outside Port Said.

'Funny,' he said. 'Unless it's just on account o' gyppo tummy. Which I doubt. Everyone gets gyppo tummy, first time through.'

'What d'you think, then?'

'Bloody anything's likely. Dysentery, I s'pose, yellow fever –'

'Not in Egypt. Yellow fever's West Africa – Freetown.'

'All right. Well, typhus.' Then Ramm put his finger on it. 'Cholera. But they can inoculate against all them perishing diseases now, can't they.'

'I reckon so, yes.' Perryman belched. 'You been done, have you?'

'No. Only TABT back in Pompey.'

'Me too, in Chatham. Nothing about cholera. Funny! That quack didn't say anything about lining up for jabs, did he, on the tannoy?'

'Probably left it all behind on the Clyde,' Ramm said with his customary cynicism.

iii

Ramm didn't know how right he'd been. The reason the RAMC doctor had made no mention of cholera jabs over the tannoy was simply because there were none available. There had been a military cock-up; the supplies that should have been put aboard the troopship off Greenock from the base hospital at Netley on Southampton Water had never arrived, and the absence had not been perceived until after the news of the outbreak had come aboard in Alexandria, when preparations were about to be put in hand for a mass inoculation process. By that time the army's hygiene officer had gone ashore; when contacted, he refused point-blank to supply the ship from the shore stocks. He had his outfit to think about, and that outfit

56

was a very large one and was poised for a breakthrough against Rommel. He was very sorry but there it was: he couldn't deprive the army in North Africa just to plug the hole left by inefficiency and failure to check stocks and indents. Monty, for one – and a very important one – would never permit it. HQ would be in touch with Port Said, and, it was hoped, a consignment would be put aboard whilst the *Orlando* was awaiting canal entry.

Dr Crampton, during the run from Alex, sought a consultation with the Master. He said, 'I have a small stock, sir. Ship's supplies.'

'Not enough for the troops?'

'Far from it,' Crampton said. 'We were relying on the army as always.'

'Enough for our own ship's company?'

'Not all of them, no.'

'Why's that, Doctor?'

Crampton said, 'Because I found I had a mostly dud batch. I'm afraid I didn't discover that until this morning. I'm taking the first opportunity of reporting it, sir.'

Bracewell was icy. 'How dud?'

'Dud enough to be useless, or worse, dangerous.' Crampton went into an involved exposition of how cholera antitoxin should be stored, the relevance of date stamping and so on, but Bracewell cut him short.

'It's done now and we're landed with it, but for God's sake, I've never come up against quite such a medical balls-up!'

'I'm sorry –'

'All right, Doctor. What do you suggest in the bloody wretched circumstances?'

'I suggest I inoculate key personnel, sir.'

'That's going to look good to the unfortunates, isn't it!'

'Needs must, sir. There are men we can't do without. You for one.'

'You can leave me out of it.'

'With respect, sir – no. That's just not on. If you went down with it – well, I needn't say more. Then the Commodore, the Staff Captain, chief engineer, chief steward say, as many deck and engineer officers as possible . . . and OC Troops and his orderly room staff.' Crampton paused. 'It's the best we can do now, sir. I repeat, I'm very sorry.'

'What about the naval party, and the girls? We'll need the gunners, all the way through.'

'Yes, sir. There should be enough. But it's going to be a case of priorities.'

Bracewell blew out his breath. He was furiously angry but there was nothing to be done about it. Except one thing. He said, 'I'll see what we can raise from the escort. *Glamorgan* may be able to help out. I'll talk to you again later, Doctor.'

'Yes, sir. In the meantime, I'll get everything ready.'

As Crampton saluted and turned to leave the bridge, Bracewell stopped him. 'Just one thing more. How long before the jabs take effect? What I'm getting at is, are we already too late in fact?'

'No, that's all right, there's still time. I wouldn't expect anything to show for quite a few days, and then only in perhaps one or two cases. But, frankly, I have to say that the cholera vaccine isn't terribly effective anyway.' Crampton went below to make his preparations with Mary McCann: she and he would each inoculate the other. Neither of them saw this as queue-jumping: the *Orlando* was going to need all the doctors and nurses available.

iv

From the bridge, Kemp watched the familiar scenes slide past – the bumboats, now being kept well clear of the ship's side by the bosun and his party with fire hoses, the occupants shaking their fists at the white infidels who were ruining their customary trade in cheap trinkets, fruit, corn cures – anything that used to sell to the peacetime liner passengers. The store of Simon Artz on the waterfront to starboard – Simon Artz where, on a larger scale than the bumboats, you could buy almost anything you fancied from a desert outfit, an Indian carpet or a case of the best champagne, to strings of cheap beads and useless mementoes of Port Said. Standing ready to take any signals the Commodore might wish to make to the port authorities, Yeoman Lambert looked across at Simon Artz, and looked with bitterness and regret. The last time he'd passed through the canal had been in peacetime, years ago, when he'd been in a light cruiser under orders for Singapore to join the East Indies. He'd gone ashore and at Simon Artz he'd bought that french letter. A packet to be honest, but he'd given the others to needy messmates. It was a wonder his hadn't rotted.

It just showed, he thought sadly. So bloody old, and never used. If only the missus could be persuaded to believe that . . .

Kemp stood like a statue, feeling cold inside. Bracewell had given him the facts of the ship's antitoxin supply. He had been persuaded to take the inoculation: his duty, Bracewell had insisted. The Admiralty, he knew, would say exactly the same. But he didn't like any of it. He felt he was setting himself up as a kind of God, deciding his own fate and to hell with the unlucky ones. By now all the senior officers had had their jabs, except the Captain himself and those deck officers also required for duty until the ship was into the canal proper. So the brass would be safe. That they were so was being kept dark, for obvious reasons.

The signal had been made requesting urgent supplies of anti-cholera vaccine. As Kemp and Bracewell had expected the answer had been a decided no. The ship was moving out of the danger zone; the local inhabitants and the British military and naval personnel were held to the port and must have protection.

No help anywhere; but they'd asked for it, Kemp thought. He was in a savage mood. This convoy had not been a good one at all. Never in all his seafaring experience had Kemp had to contend with a serious epidemic aboard a ship. Minor ones, yes – the various stomach upsets that could strike and spread rapidly, flu and allied upsets, even measles among the children, or chicken pox. But never cholera.

Cholera, in the close confines of an over-crowded troop transport with no ability to mount anything approaching a full-scale inoculation. Of course, it hadn't happened yet. Maybe it never would. But Kemp felt in his bones that it was going to. There seemed to be a jonah around.

Flies . . .

Kemp swatted at them. Port Said was the home of flies, they were everywhere. Filthy, bloodsucking brutes, crawling over men and refuse – over food. Their legions would be below in the *Orlando*'s accommodation already, with their horrible hairy legs to which refuse from the gutters of the port could have stuck. They could spread the disease presumably, the dreaded disease that from time to time ravaged India and China and the Nile delta among other places. They were not going to escape it.

V

RSM Pollock, Bull's Bollocks to his soldiers, was taking a look at Port Said through the orderly room porthole. He had passed this way before, one of the very few of the troops who had, on draft for Indian service aboard a pre-war trooper bound for Bombay. He knew a thing or two about cholera. In the old days of the North-West Frontier fighting, it had hit the regiments hard at times, very hard. Death by the dozen. Today they could fight it better, but it was still a real dirty threat. RSM Pollock, one of the senior warrant officers who'd had to be put in the picture, reflected on the lack of jabs. Bad, that.

He looked sideways as Captain Archer came in.

'Well, Mr Pollock.'

Pollock kept his face blank. 'Well Mr Pollock' was just the sort of meaningless remark you came to expect from Captain Archer. He said, 'Very well, sir, thank you. So far.'

'Yes, quite. It's nasty.'

'Sooner die with the enemy in front of me, sir, and running. But it's not for us to decide, sir, all said and done. We take what comes.'

'It may not come, you know, Mr Pollock.'

'No, sir, indeed it may not, and I know that. But the cholera has nasty habits, sir. As that Rudyard Kipling knew, sir.'

'Kipling?'

'A poet, sir –'

60

'I know of him, Mr Pollock. Jolly good stuff!'

'Then you'll know what he wrote about the cholera, sir.' RSM Pollock didn't wait for a reply. He quoted, ' "There aren't much comfort 'andy on ten deaths a day." You know it, sir?'

'Not all –'

'Then allow me, sir. What Kipling wrote was this: "We've got the cholera in camp – it's worse than forty fights; we're dyin' in the wilderness the same as Isrulites. It's before us an' be'ind us, an' we cannot get away, an' the doctor's just reported we've ten more today." Sir!'

'Ah . . .'

'Mark what the poet said, sir. "We cannot get away." '

SIX

There was a delay in Port Said, not for the first time in the canal's history; no-one was quite sure why – again, not for the first time. Egyptian officials usually caused delays and it was often said that they did so in order to enhance their own importance. In Bracewell's wartime experience, much the same could be said of the army. This time the belief was that both the Egyptians and the army in concert were responsible. In the event it was towards dark when the canal pilot embarked and was taken to the bridge.

Bracewell asked him what it had all been about.

'Shortage of pilots, sir. There's a lot of us stuck at the other end, in Suez.'

Bracewell snorted. 'Surely I could have been told?'

'They never give anything away, Captain.'

'In case it leaks to Berlin, I suppose.' Bracewell, like Kemp and all the other bridge personnel, swatted at the swarms of flies. 'Well – let's get on with it, then. She's yours, pilot.'

'Right, sir.' The canal pilot was British; there were an equal number of British and French pilots, all of them with master mariner's certificates and the majority of them ex-liner officers well used to the canal passage before they joined the pilotage service. Many Orient, P & O and Mediterranean–Australia Line officers had transferred to the canal company, mostly the married ones seeking more home life and the closer proximity of their wives. Neither Bracewell nor Kemp had sailed with the present pilot but there was always a lot of trust between the liner masters and the pilots. As his ship moved at dead slow for the canal entry, the last signals made to and from the port authority, Bracewell wondered what it would be like if ever the Egyptians took control of the canal and eased out the British and French pilots. Already, before the war, there had been a veiled hostility from the natives, and contemptuous gestures along the canal banks as the peasantry had watched the passage of the liners, so close at times to the banks.

It was in fact evident again now, despite the fading light. PO Wren Hardisty was looking from her cabin port, head thrust out to catch a breath of air to relieve the stifling conditions below decks, when she caught sight of a group of Egyptian labourers quite close as the troopship moved past. They seemed to her to be wearing garments like nightdresses, long and flowing, some of them white, some of them striped. Funny, she thought, but there was no accounting for foreigners.

Then, as though a signal had been given, there was a stir. The nightdresses were lifted high. There was a chorus of yells, and laughter, and indescribable things were taken in hand and waved towards the ship.

'Well, I never!' Miss Hardisty said, shocked to the core. Her face scarlet, she withdrew from the port and banged the glass and deadlight shut.

ii

Further inoculations had taken place. The Commodore's staff and the ship's own gunnery rates had had their jabs. The women, the WRNS draft, had not. Dr Crampton had been the arbiter of the priorities, and he had felt it his duty to give that priority to essential personnel, which the Wrens were not. Had it not been for the surgeon commander aboard the *Glamorgan*, even the gunners would not have been protected. The flagship had her own ship's company to consider, and the surplus had not been great. The surgeon commander had been forthcoming about inefficiency and Crampton, on his begging mission, had been mortified as he'd listened to a blistering tirade. Then, when he reported to the bridge, Commodore Kemp had hit the roof. To put women at risk was sheerly criminal. The Commodore, already briefed on the way the disease was transmitted, had asked for a full run-down on the symptoms and the general course the cholera would take.

Crampton gave it to him, after, once again making the point that the vaccine was not always effective.

'It usually starts with diarrhoea, sir. That alone makes it hard to diagnose in the first instance. It can easily be mistaken for plain gyppo tummy –'

'But not this time, Doctor.'

'Not this time, sir. We've had the warning.' Crampton paused. 'Then there's vomiting, feeble circulation, coldness, cramps. Then perhaps collapse. Anyone whose intestines have been weakened by previous illness, or poor feeding, or are just very tired . . . they're the most at risk. Also overeating and drinking don't help.'

'The progress is fairly rapid, isn't it?'

Crampton nodded. 'It can be, sir. In just a few hours the stools develop the characteristics – a sort of rice-water appearance, thin and watery and colourless except that they carry quantities of white particles like rice. These are shreds of intestinal mucous membrane that have become detached. The body's surface becomes very cold, though the temperature of the actual intestine rises way above normal. The patient gets severe cramp in the limbs and is then likely to go into complete collapse, not able to help himself in any way, though usually he remains mentally aware, quite clear-headed. The mouth and throat go very dry . . . this and the general physical weakness make the voice low and hoarse. That's known as the *vox cholerica*. And the breath becomes cold.'

'Is that the last stage?'

'It can be and often is. But if a favourable reaction takes place, the patient goes into a natural sleep, a deep one, and then there can be a rapid recovery. On the other hand, if the reaction's not complete, there can be a relapse into a typhoid state, that's to say a condition resembling typhoid fever though it's not strictly typhoid.'

'And the prognosis after that?'

'Fifty-fifty. The attack *can* start and end in less than twelve hours – death or recovery. That's the actual cholera . . . but if there is this typhoid state, it can be up to around ten days before death. If the patient holds out beyond that, well, one can expect recovery.'

'Expect?'

'Yes, sir. It's by no means certain.'

'You've talked more of death than recovery, Doctor.'

'That's often the way of it, sir.'

'And that's what those girls have to face. I think that's diabolical.'

'I'm sorry –'

Kemp held up a hand. 'All right, Doctor. I'll say no more. I know you'll be doing your best and that's what counts now.'

iii

Petty Officer Perryman was in a state of jitters, Ramm saw. On their first meeting off Malta Ramm had put his fellow gunner's mate down as a hypochondriac without, then, any real reason for doing so. It had been just an impression because of the anxious look on his face whenever he did one of his belches, as though he feared for the basic condition of his gut. Now the hypochondria was coming out, and the ship barely into the canal.

'Bloody flies,' Perryman said, swatting wildly. 'Got crap on their feet, they have. Gyppo crap.'

'Not worried yet, are you?'

'Course I am! So should you be. First sign o' the squitters, and I'm off to the quack double quick.'

'Well, I s'pose you can't be too careful.'

'Course you can't. Stands to reason, nip it quick and you got a chance.'

Ramm scratched beneath his chin. He reckoned they were safe enough, having had the inoculation. But Perryman wasn't so sure. Inoculation, he said, didn't always work. He'd known a bloke in Freetown, Sierra Leone, at the start of the war when the naval base had been set up for the escorts of the South Atlantic convoys. Been inoculated against everything under the sun, the bloke had – blackwater fever, yellow fever as well as TABT – and went down with yellow fever. 'Pegged out inside the week,' Perryman said in an aggrieved tone. 'Bloody mosquitos, see.'

'Nothing like looking on the bright side,' Ramm said.

'Stuff that! With all these perishing flies?'

Ramm left him to it and went below, where the troops were still battened down. The air was thick, stifling. Sweat poured; the troop decks were hell. The stench from them seemed to spread throughout the ship. So did something else, something even more pervasive, as the day's orderly officer, having made his rounds, reported to the brigade major in the orderly room.

'The smell of fear, Major.'

The brigade major lit a cigarette and blew smoke. 'Don't be melodramatic, old boy.'

'I'm not, sir. It's real enough.' The orderly officer's khaki-drill was dark with great patches of sweat. 'It's not all that surprising, is it? Battened down below with no air and the threat of cholera! There's a feeling of claustrophobia around and that's not good. I tell you, I didn't like it.'

The brigade major shrugged. 'They'll have to put up with it for another – what – 12 hours at least.'

'Could be 12 hours too long, sir.'

'H'm? What are you suggesting, old boy?'

The answer came without hesitation. 'Trouble.'

'Mutiny? Don't be –'

'Not full scale mutiny, no. But there could be a break-out from confinement, which some people might see as a sort of mutiny.' The orderly officer paused, tapping his cane against a thigh. 'OC Troops for one. And if he reacted, well, it would be damned unfair.'

The brigade major was about to speak again when the sound of briskly marching footsteps was heard along the alleyway outside and RSM Pollock entered and slammed to attention.

'Stand easy, please, Mr Pollock.'

66

'Sir!'

'You've appeared at an opportune moment, Mr Pollock.' The brigade major repeated what the orderly officer had been saying. 'What's your view, Mr Pollock?'

Pollock blew out his cheeks. 'My view, sir, is that I shall go and take a look. If there's to be trouble, sir, it'll not last long. With your permission, sir.'

'Of course, Mr Pollock, of course.'

RSM Pollock gave a swinging salute and turned about with a crash of boots. The brigade major murmured a remark that such parade-ground activity seemed out of place aboard a ship, but Pollock, on his way out of the orderly room, didn't hear. He marched along the alleyway, down the main staircase towards the troop decks. Going lower in the ship, the pong, the staleness, grew worse and Pollock felt as though he were advancing into a steam bath or such. Entering the troop deck and its clouds of cigarette smoke he marched slowly along the aisles between the bunks, saying nothing but eyeing the men, who stood to attention as he passed by. All except for three men, one a lance-corporal, of the RASC. These men, lounging on their bunks in a swelter of perspiration, stayed put.

RSM Pollock halted. 'You,' he said. He pointed his cane at the lance-corporal. 'On your feet, laddie, sharp!'

The lance-corporal, taking it deliberately slowly, stood up. 'Me, sir?'

'Who else?'

The lance-corporal failed to meet the RSM's eye; he glanced aside, saw the other two men get to their feet as well. Pollock said, 'Slackness will not be tolerated. Watch that chevron, laddie.'

'It's the conditions, sir.'

'Aha.' RSM Pollock, like a policeman resting from the beat, rocked a little back and forth on the balls of his feet. 'Makes you tired, do they? The conditions?'

'Yes.'

'Yes, sir.'

'Yes, sir.'

'That's better. What a shame that you feel tired. I am so

sorry. So do I feel tired, seeing after such as you. Day after day! That gives me a very great feeling that I want to lie down and die, so tired do I get. But I stays on my feet because there's a war on. So do you. Do I make myself clear, laddie?'

'Yes, sir.' The tone was surly, but RSM Pollock disregarded it. He turned about and marched back to the entry to the troop deck, where once again he turned and raised his voice loudly. 'Now listen to me, all you men. You're hot and smelly. I know that. So do the officers. Breathing's a torture. I know that too. I know, because I've been this way before, that when a boat's in the Suez Canal not much fresh air comes down the ventilators. Can't, when the boat's moving slow. But the canal doesn't go on forever – not it. Once we're clear, things'll improve. Meanwhile, the orders are the orders and remain so. No men to show on deck. It may sound daft but there's sense behind it. We don't want Hitler to know we're here. And whatever you think you know about that, the high command knows better. All right?'

A voice, an unknown one from half-way along the central bank of bunks, said, 'Sod the air. What about the cholera?'

There was a chorus of agreement.

RSM Pollock raised his voice again, quelling a hubbub. 'Yes, the cholera. I don't deny that's bad. But moaning won't help. And the conditions down here won't make the chances of the cholera any worse. The doctor's already broadcast, right? It's not caught by contact. It's not caught by breath. It's not caught by someone sneezing in your face. Care with the latrines, cleansing with carbolic as already ordered, that does the trick. You don't need to worry about the cholera. Not any more than if you was on deck.' RSM Pollock paused. 'Any specific complaints, genuine complaints, put them to your platoon sergeants and they'll go to the orderly room for consideration. I can't say fairer than that.'

Pollock turned to make his way to the remaining troop decks and repeat his performance. When he was a short distance off he heard the sound of singing. With it someone was playing a squeeze box. The words followed him, loud and clear. *'When this bloody war is over, Oh how happy I shall be . . . no more bashing the parade ground, no more asking for a pass . . . I shall tell the sergeant-major to shove his warrant up his arse.'*

68

Mr Pollock gave a sharp tug to the front of his khaki-drill tunic and went on his way. After making the rounds of all the troop decks, and hearing from each something similar by way of song to mark his departure, he returned to the orderly room to report the soldiers behaving much as might be expected. No trouble, he said. Just a handful of skrimshankers here and there.

iv

For the catering staff, as well as for the medics, the day had been a busy one. There were so many arrangements to make, so many precautions to be put in hand, and not only put in hand but checked continually to make 100 percent sure the orders were acted upon. As Purser Rhys-Jones remarked to the chief steward, it was a case of life and death.

'I've seen it before, Mr Bliss. Cholera.'

'You have, sir?'

Rhys-Jones nodded. 'Not in this company. Years ago, when I was an assistant purser with Hiley Fergusson Lines, cruise ships. Here in Egypt it was. The passengers went on a shore excursion to the pyramids; that's where it came from, I think. Some dirty food perhaps, or maybe it was the flies, you know. You should not allow the flies to settle on your lips, tell your stewards. They are dirty things. Well, the first cases hit us just as we reached the Bitter Lakes, and it was very bad, very bad indeed.'

'Many dead, sir?' Chief Steward Bliss asked.

'Oh yes. They nearly all died. The doctor, I am afraid, was not up to it. There was a big fuss in the papers, I can tell you, and the company got much of the blame.'

Bliss said, 'I reckon I remember hearing about it, sir –'

'Yes, I am sure you did, and I was there, you see. So now we must be very careful.' Rhys-Jones wagged a finger. 'Once bitten, you know, twice shy, isn't it? So you will make sure everyone does his duty and attends to the instructions from the doctors.'

'I'll do that all right, sir.' Bliss had gone down to his office with sheaves of instructions in his head to talk it over with his deputy, the second steward. Of course, it wasn't like having a ship full of passengers all in a state of twitter. The army was responsible for the troop decks; but the ship's crew was the chief steward's worry to a large extent. There were the lavatories, which had to be kept scrupulously clean since they could be the main source of transmission of the cholera. A lot of carbolic would have to be used. There would have to be the greatest care in the washing of cups and dishes, knives and forks and so on. And then there were the galleys, where the food for all on board, the army included, was prepared and cooked. Vegetables to be washed in permanganate of potassium; meat to be very carefully cooked, everything to be protected from the flies. Water for drinking to be boiled, likewise milk, and fruit to be off the menu until they could obtain fresh supplies in Aden at the bottom end of the Red Sea, some days ahead after clearing away from Suez, which itself wouldn't be until latish next day. While they were in the canal the whole catering department would be fully instructed as ordered by the purser, who had had his orders from the Staff Captain personally.

v

Kemp left the bridge after the ship had anchored in the Great Bitter Lake to allow the northward passage of the convoy coming up from Suez: two lines of ships could not pass in the narrow confines of the canal proper, and a wait was necessary in the wider waters of the Bitter Lakes. Kemp went below to his cabin for a salt-water bath and a change of clothing: he was sticky with sweat and felt his mouth to be full of dust. After the bath he felt more human, and settled the dust with a whisky and soda. He believed he could allow himself that; there was not likely to be any emergency in the Bitter Lakes, though perhaps a sortie of bombers from Crete couldn't be entirely discounted. Just because of that possibility the whisky was weak. He had drained his glass when a knock came on his doorpost.

'Come in,' he called.

It was Jean Forrest. 'I hope I'm not intruding, Commodore?'

'By no means. Care for a drink – gin?'

She shook her head. 'I won't, thank you. I've been hearing rumours, medical ones.' She smiled rather tiredly. 'Those who drink are the most likely to get it, Commodore.'

Kemp laughed. 'Drink means just that – drink. Boozers, Miss Forrest. Not us.'

'No. I know, but still. I won't. Don't let me stop you.'

'I won't have more than the one. What's up?'

She said, 'Nothing's up. I'm just being a nuisance, I'm afraid. It's . . . really not the hour for calling, is it?'

'Never mind, Miss Forrest. Something's bothering you. Is it your young ladies?'

'Yes,' she said, 'it is. I've been pretty worried. This business of no inoculations –'

'I know. That's unforgivable. Someone's going to get it in the neck, you can be sure.'

'That won't help us for now, Commodore.'

Suddenly Kemp realized he hadn't asked her to sit down. He did so and apologized for his manners. 'I'm not much of a drawing-room man, Miss Forrest.'

She smiled. He saw that she was studying him and he felt a flash of annoyance because he didn't like being looked at in the light of a specimen, but he knew she was concerned about him and he knew he was beginning to look exceptionally tired and strained. There was even a shake in his fingers as he offered her a cigarette and lit both it and his own. Age, he supposed; or recent stress was perhaps more likely. She went on, 'I suppose there's no reason why it should come aboard at all.'

'No reason at all. The only contact with the shore has been the pilot. Oh, and the other shore people, of course. Not very many of them and they all looked clean to me. Don't worry till it happens, that's my advice.'

She gave him another close look. 'You've been worrying,' she said. 'You've not been taking your own advice.'

'No,' he said flatly. 'No, I dare say I haven't. But I do know it doesn't do any good, and anyway it's not just the damn

71

cholera I have to worry about. There's – there's . . .' His voice faltered a little, to his own surprise. He covered it with a cough; he was much embarrassed. 'Well, never mind, Miss Forrest. You've come for reassurance, not to hear me moan.'

She said, 'You could do with getting it all off your chest, Commodore. I'm not really asking for reassurance – I know there isn't any you can give. We just have to face up to it if it comes, that's all.'

Kemp put his face in his hands for a moment. Everything was catching up: the long-drawn-out war, the months of keeping the seas, the long absences from his wife and the cottage in Meopham in Kent where – unlikely dependant at his age – he still maintained his nonagenarian grandmother who had brought him up on his mother's early death and who he knew was a never-ending drain on Mary his wife. Two sons at sea in the destroyers, the constant worry about them at the back of his mind. The responsibilities of a convoy commodore, so many men looking to him for a lead when the convoys came under attack from aircraft, submarines or surface vessels. Often appalling weather conditions, especially in the North Atlantic and on the terrible run to Murmansk in North Russia to help keep Stalin's armies supplied and fighting on. And now the filthy threat of cholera – largely because there had been that criminal neglect of duty to provide enough vaccine to inoculate all personnel.

He dropped his hands and gave a short, hard laugh. He said, 'Yes, we'll face up to it. As you suggested, Miss Forrest, we take what comes. And we come up smiling . . . more or less! Never say die – isn't that what they say?'

Jean Forrest nodded. In a soft voice she said, 'You're a good man, Commodore Kemp. A dependable one. And now I'd better go and get some sleep. I hope you will too.'

Kemp stood for a long while looking at the cabin curtain through which she had gone. Then he stripped off his white uniform shirt with the broad gold band of a commodore RNR on the shoulder straps. That gold band meant a lot; he had to live up to it. He stiffened himself, regretting a moment of weakness in front of a first officer WRNS. He admitted the truth to himself: he was scared of the cholera and of what it could turn a ship into. Fighting the enemy was one thing; fighting a disgusting bug was quite another.

He turned into his bunk.

vi

After the northbound convoy had passed through, the southbound one weighed anchor and moved on towards Suez. The escorting cruisers and destroyers were in the lead, with the armaments carriers between them and the flagship *Glamorgan* bringing up the rear. The night had been close, hot, foetid below decks; after the dawn came the searing sun to make matters worse. Those on the bridge and in exposed positions sweltered. From the guns Petty Officer Ramm looked along decks that, being virtually deserted, appeared strangely unfamiliar. Until just before Alex, those decks had swarmed with troops. Ramm reckoned it was a load of old codswallop, keeping the brown jobs below, that wasn't going to fool Hitler, not likely! But the ways of the brass were always weird and inexplicable. Officers were a rum bunch to start with, used different terms, talked different. Where for instance the ship's company always called the coxswain of a destroyer the swain, officers called him the cox'n. Officers spoke of leave, the ratings of leaf, or anyway masters-at-arms and regulating petty officers, the ship's police, did. Lots of things like that to differentiate. Officers spoke of the old light cruiser *Caradoc* with the accent on the second 'a', the lower deck put the emphasis on the 'o', unless they were cw ratings, those up for commissions, when they used the officers' pronunciation. Ramm, thus reflecting when he was approached by Perryman, spoke his thoughts aloud.

'Wouldn't get a bloody commission else,' po Perryman said with certainty. He rubbed at his eyes and swatted at the merciless, unending flies. 'Talking o' which . . . couple o' years back I was gunner's mate o' the commodore's guard in RNB Chats. Every third day, we did duty on the cell block, looking after the blokes doing –'

73

'Yes, I know,' Ramm interrupted. 'I'm not all green when it comes to that.'

'Sorry. Well, anyway, one night, I calls down the cell alleyway towards the OD on guard, who I couldn't see cos 'e was round the corner, right? 'E answers in a posh accent and I was took flat aback, thinking an officer had got down there.' Perryman sucked at his teeth. 'Know what? I called the little bleeder sir. 'E was one of them cw blokes. I could 'ave pissed myself, after, when 'e come in sight.'

Ramm laughed. 'One thing,' he said. 'The officers'll get the cholera with the rest of us. All on a level like . . . germs don't respect gold braid.'

The convoy moved on. Ramm saw Kemp in the starboard wing of the bridge, with Bracewell and the Staff Captain. He fancied they looked worried. Ramm flapped at his shirt, getting some air between it and his skin as the day's heat increased. The ships were moving faster now; more air should be penetrating below decks. Not long after, they came up to Suez and the canal company's buildings lining the bank. Ramm went below to the heads: his bowels felt loose. He sat there a long while, dead scared. Then he went along fast to the surgery, where he found Sister McCann. Mary McCann reported to the ship's surgeon.

'Diarrhoea, Doctor. Just the one case.'

'So far. Any other symptoms?'

'No.'

'So we make tests. And pray, Mary.'

SEVEN

Ramm was the first of many. The many became a flood, most of them being in fact the troops attending the RAMC surgery, men who hadn't been through the canal until now. Also some of the WRNS, who likewise hadn't been through before. That one fact tended to make Crampton and the army medical officers believe it was just a simple case of gyppo tummy. Except for Ramm, who was not by any means doing his first trip through; generally speaking, it was only that first trip through that caught people out; after that, they acquired an immunity. But Ramm, as a result of the tests, didn't show any sign of cholera any more than did the others.

Crampton said, 'He'll have to be watched, Mary. A simple precaution.' He told Ramm to report to the surgery twice daily but not to consider himself relieved of any duties. He was probably perfectly all right. Ramm went away feeling happier and spoke to Perryman, whose gut seemed to be behaving normally. That worried Ramm; why didn't Perryman have the squitters, with his rotten gut and all, yet he did?

Crampton made his report to the Master. 'Normal so far as I can say, sir. The proportions are about the same as peacetime and all the tests have been negative.'

'Think we're in the clear?' Bracewell asked.

'No, sir, I don't. It's much too early to say that.'

Bracewell sighed. 'All right, Doctor. Keep watching.'

'I will, of course. I'll say this much – I'm fairly hopeful. We've taken every possible precaution with food and water.'

'Flies?'

'They're the weak spot, sir. But we're doing all we can against them.'

'Dirty little beasts,' Bracewell said. 'Look after yourself, Doctor.'

'Oh, I'm not irreplaceable, sir. The army has plenty of medics.' Dr Crampton excused himself and went below to his surgery. The place was empty now of all but Mary McCann, who was busy re-arranging bottles and packets of swabs and all the other paraphernalia of a surgery. Crampton gave her a close, searching look.

'All right, Mary? You look white. Anything up?'

'I don't know,' she said. 'I hope not.'

'You'd better tell me. If you're off colour, we don't want –'

She said abruptly, 'I've just vomited, Doctor.'

'H'm. Diarrhoea?'

'Yes,' she said. She looked close to tears, Crampton thought. 'There'll have to be tests, of course. But I'll carry on. I can't infect anybody.'

'No,' Crampton said. 'No, you can't, Mary.' They both knew that to be a fact. But there was something else that had equally to be accepted as a fact. The lay mind was not going to believe she couldn't be infectious and when it became obvious that the ship's nursing sister wasn't well there could be a panic. He said, 'I'll have to put you off duty at once, Mary, if the tests show anything. I'm not having you putting yourself at risk. And that's final – doctor's orders!'

'Let's get on with the tests,' she said. She was putting a brave face on it but they both knew the score: if she'd got it she wouldn't be able to carry on. It was the early cases in a cholera epidemic that were often the worst, and the disease moved very fast in the body once established.

ii

Rounds again, after the convoy had cleared from the canal and the *Orlando* was moving through the Gulf of Suez towards the wider waters of the Red Sea. The usual retinue followed

76

behind the troopship's Staff Captain and Brigadier Pumphrey-Hatton, the latter looking edgy as he made his way along the troop decks, making great play with a handkerchief doused with eau-de-cologne, touching it now and again to his nostrils.

He emerged into the open deck aft. 'Damn smelly,' he said to the brigade major.

'Very, sir.'

'Don't know how they put up with it really. Great self-control. Damned if I'd like it. Did you notice anything else, Major?'

The brigade major said cautiously, 'If you mean the atmosphere – the sweat apart again – yes, I did, sir.'

'Brittle.'

'Yes, sir.' The brigade major was surprised that Pumphrey-Hatton had noticed anything; usually, he didn't. It was also surprising that he'd spoken more or less sympathetically about what the soldiers were enduring. Again, usually he didn't. As for the atmosphere, the emanation of surliness along the troop decks, it was there all right and must have grown worse since RSM Pollock had made his report. The brigade major was about to speak again when OC Troops cut him short.

'They'll just have to put up with it, Major.' That was more like Pumphrey-Hatton. 'Where are we now?'

'Still in the Gulf of Suez, sir.'

'Ah, yes. Damned hot!'

'Once we're clear of the Gulf, we'll be well out of sight from the land, sir.'

'Yes. What you're saying is, the men can come out on deck again. Well – we shall see.'

'But surely –'

'Thank you, Brigade Major. What I said was, we shall see.'

'Very good, sir.'

Rounds dispersed, the various officers and senior NCOS going about their duties. Pumphrey-Hatton went to his stateroom, the spacious accommodation rivalling the Master's, the special suite that in peacetime had carried the most important, or most noble, or simply the richest family in

77

the passenger list. Lord Nuffield had travelled frequently in the *Orlando*; the husband of Amy Johnson the air ace had gone by Orient Line to Sydney; dukes and earls had sailed in her; admirals taking up or relinquishing appointments on loan to the Royal Australian Navy had walked the liner's decks and sat at the Captain's table in the saloon. Today the honour and glory were all Pumphrey-Hatton's. He was very comfortable and had an excellent batman who worked with a steward from the liner's catering department to minister to the needs of oc Troops. Loosening his khaki-drill tunic Pumphrey- Hatton ordered a long gin-and-lemon with ice. Thinking of how damnable it was down below in the troop decks, Pumphrey-Hatton drank and felt a great deal better.

Then he looked again at his glass, now almost empty. There was a speck on the inside. Frowning, he looked at it closely: could it be a fly-blow? He believed it was; and the ice could have been from contaminated water, you never knew, there was inevitably carelessness around. Somebody was going to suffer for this.

Pumphrey-Hatton called loudly for his batman and steward.

iii

It was in fact another six hours after clearing from the Gulf of Suez that oc Troops passed the word that the men could be allowed on deck. This was as a result of representations from the battalion commanders, to whom in the interval RSM Pollock had reported in no uncertain terms.

'I smell trouble, gentlemen. Men at the end of their tethers. The troop decks, gentlemen, are diabolical. You'll have noticed that there's a following wind.'

That had been noted; the wind, a hot one, was blowing directly against the wind made by the ship's own passage, and the two forces were negating each other. The result aboard the ship was a state of windlessness. No air was going down the ventilators. Below, it was a case of swelter, with everything – uniforms, bedding – soaked in sweat. The general effect was that of a kettle on a hob; heated by the sun from above, the ship's plates were heated by the sea from below. RSM Pollock went on, 'If you ask me, gentlemen, there could be a breakout.'

'You really think it's come to that, do you?'

'That's my view, sir. I do think that. It has worsened a great deal, sir, since I went round the troop decks last night. If I may make the point, sir, when the War Office issued the instruction, there was not a cholera epidemic.'

The point was taken. The three battalion commanders waited upon OC Troops in his stateroom. They put the point strongly. To carry on the charade any longer was farcical.

'Charade, Colonel?'

'That was my word, sir.'

'It's not that of the War Office.'

'The War Office doesn't live on the troop deck, sir.'

'There's no need to be impertinent!' Pumphrey-Hatton snapped. Then he seemed to go off at a tangent. He took a few jerky turns up and down the day cabin then swung round on the three senior officers. 'I had some damn fly dirt in my gin this morning. That's serious. Or could be. I won't have all this damned carelessness, it's very worrying. And I do see . . . yes, all right. Pass the word that the soldiers can come on deck. Make sure it's done in an orderly fashion. No scrambling.'

Looks were exchanged as the colonels left the stateroom. The word was passed. The senior NCOs of the brigade stood by the exits from the troop decks. RSM Pollock stationed himself at the after end of the main alleyway from the ship's interior, another warrant officer taking the for'ard exit. The men came out like a tidal wave, shouting and cheering, a stampede that couldn't wait to gulp down air. In the mêlée RSM Pollock was biffed by an elbow and swung round like a top before falling to the deck. A number of feet passed over him before he was able to wriggle out of the main stream. When the mob had gone, he clambered to his feet, his khaki-drill filthy, his cap crushed, his cane gone he knew not where.

The air became blue. Then he was addressed by a large plump woman wearing a Wren's hat and blue crossed anchors on the left sleeve of her white blouse.

'Such language in front of a lady! I never did hear the like,' Miss Hardisty said. 'You ought to be thoroughly ashamed of yourself!'

It was not Miss Hardisty's lucky day: she was in for worse. One of her Wrens was also in the vicinity, a young girl of nineteen. Miss Hardisty was gently upbraided. 'Did you know who that was, PO?'

'No, and I don't –'

'Mr Pollock.' The silly girl giggled and looked coy. 'They call him Bull's Bollocks.'

iv

Kemp looked down once again on full decks, a sea of khaki. He was glad and relieved to see it. The order had been inhuman, but it wasn't for him to query the dictates of the War Office or the military command. There was already that coldness between himself and OC Troops, an unwelcome state of affairs. He paced the bridge with Sub-Lieutenant Finnegan and got rid of some of his feelings.

'About time, Finnegan. Typical army, I call it. Constipated minds, h'm?'

'If you say so, sir.'

Kemp glared. 'I just have. What's that remark supposed to mean?'

'Just that I wouldn't criticize the British Army, sir.'

'Ah. Because you're an American?'

'I guess so, sir.'

'Feel free, Finnegan.'

'You mean that, sir?'

'I don't usually say what I don't mean, Finnegan.'

'Okay, sir, okay.' There was a gleam in the sub's eye. 'In that case, sir, I reckon that OC Troops is a stuffed shirt with a pea brain and a –'

'That's *too* free, Finnegan. But to use your own words – if you say so.'

Finnegan grinned. 'I guess we're in accord after all.'

'I guess the same. But never whisper it elsewhere,

Finnegan.' Kemp turned as the yeoman of signals approached, looking urgent, with a signal pad in his hand. 'Yes, Yeoman?'

'Signal from the extended escort, sir, repeated by *Guernsey*. Addressed Flag repeated Commodore, sir. Asdic contact bearing due south, sir, distance three miles.'

'*Submarine?* For God's sake . . . in the Red Sea?' The question was rhetorical; Lambert gave no answer. Kemp went at the double for the voice-pipe to the Master's cabin. Bracewell was on the bridge within thirty seconds, and by the time he got there Kemp had already pressed the action alarm. Bracewell asked, 'Where the hell have they come from, Commodore?'

'Probably Japan. Or could be U-boats having made the passage of the Cape. Fuelled from a parent tanker. But personally I go for Japs. It's a suicide mission – it has to be, in comparatively confined waters so far up. And we all know the Japs.'

Kemp was watching out ahead, binoculars to his eyes, looking for more signals. The contact was three miles ahead of the extended screen; that made it around fifteen miles ahead of the *Orlando*'s present position. A little time in hand but not much, and then there could be bloody chaos, Kemp thought, with a submarine loose among the ships of the convoy. Already Lambert on Kemp's order had passed the signal to the merchant ships, the armaments carriers; aboard them the DEMS gunners would be manning their weapons, the masters looking out as anxiously as Kemp was. Meanwhile the troopship's own gunners were doubling to their stations carrying steel helmets and white anti-flash gear for the protection of heads and faces, necks and hands. With them, Perryman and Ramm took charge of their sections fore and aft. Within two minutes, all the armament was manned and ready, awaiting firing orders from Sub-Lieutenant Finnegan on the bridge. Ramm's stomach was still playing him up. He'd been evacuating himself again when the alarm rattlers had sounded, and by now he was a very worried man though he hadn't vomited. Not yet. But just thinking about the fact that he might do so, and thus take a step nearer a diagnosis of cholera, made him feel slightly sick. But that was probably no more than imagination, a sort of auto-suggestion.

On the bridge, Kemp was still trying to make an assessment, by which he meant a guess, as to the unknown submarine's nationality. Back at the convoy conference on the Clyde, when the complete convoy had left Scottish waters for Trincomalee via Malta and Alex, there had been no mention of the likelihood of submarine attack in the Red Sea, though it was known, of course, that the Japanese naval forces were operating across the Bay of Bengal and possibly round the southern tip of India into the Indian Ocean and possibly even the Arabian Sea.

'But to come round Gardafui, Finnegan!' Gardafui was the cape at the north-eastern tip of Italian Somaliland. 'And then to come right through the Gates of Hell. That's what we call the Strait of Bab el Mandeb, this side of Aden.'

'The narrows?'

'Yes. It's unbelievable. Makes me think that contact could be a British submarine.' Kemp turned aside and called to Lambert. 'Yeoman, make to the Flag from Commodore. Have you any British submarines on the plot.'

'Yes, sir.' Lambert hesitated. 'If they had, sir, I reckon they'd have reported.'

'You'd think so, Yeoman, but cock-ups can occur and I don't want to open fire on our own side.'

'No, sir.' Lambert went across and took up his Aldis lamp. The acknowledgement came quickly from the flagship's signal bridge, and was almost immediately followed by the answer.

Lambert reported, 'Commodore from Flag, sir. Nothing of any nationality on plot but am bearing all possibilities in mind.'

'Right, Yeoman, thank you.'

At Kemp's side Bracewell said, 'If it's British, she'll surface when she's identified us.'

Kemp nodded. 'That's what I'd expect. And that's when I hope no-one's going to be trigger-happy. Unless she surfaces, I'll be expecting Captain (D) to go into the attack. After that, there won't be any further doubt.' He looked down again along the boat deck; by now the troops were at their stations on the embarkation deck below, the deck to which the lifeboats were being lowered as a precaution by the ship's crew working at the davits under the chief officer. A few moments later OC Troops came up the ladder to the bridge and approached Bracewell.

'Ah, Captain. All in hand I trust?'

'Of course,' Bracewell answered, displeased at the question.

'Don't misunderstand me. I'm not checking on you.'

'I'm glad to hear that, Brigadier.'

'It's because I had a fly-blow in my gin this morning.'

Bracewell gaped. Kemp was aware of an explosion from Finnegan. 'I beg your pardon?' Bracewell said.

'Oh, I've already blasted the steward and my own man. Disgraceful! It's carelessness, you see. Just damn carelessness. That sort of thing can spread if it's not checked very, very firmly. I thought I'd mention it.'

Bracewell said carefully, 'I shall have words with the purser, who'll speak to the chief steward. I shall have those words in due course. Currently, I have to do what I can to avoid a possible torpedo attack.'

'Quite so, yes.'

Kemp, listening, had a fleeting thought that OC Troops had had a little too much gin, fly-blown though it might have been. But his speech wasn't slurred and he was perfectly steady on his feet. Kemp decided that it must be simply the worry of the cholera. They all knew about the flies.

v

'I'm sorry, Mary,' Dr Crampton had said ten minutes before the action alarm had sounded.

'Positive?'

Crampton said, 'I'm afraid it is. You know what to do now.'

'Oh, yes, I know.' Mary McCann was shivering, though her intestinal temperature had been well above normal. 'Bed. Everything to be disinfected with carbolic acid. Then just wait for the bloody bugs to do their worst. Who's going to do the disinfecting, Doctor?'

'I'll do it myself if I have to.'

'So what's the prognosis?'

'You know as well as I do, Mary.'

'Yes,' she said, 'I suppose I do. I just want to hear you say it's not always fatal –'

'It certainly isn't. Chin up, Mary. You'll be taken very good care of. But you know that too.'

She nodded. She felt very weak, and the violent shivering was itself weakening. And the sick feeling, and the almost constant diarrhoea. Soon there would come the cramps, and then, perhaps, the state of collapse. She also knew that it was the early cases in which the disease was most virulent and that if no favourable reaction to the collapse took place then she could die within a matter of hours.

Crampton left the cabin to report to Bracewell on the bridge, adding to the Master's worries. Bracewell asked, 'Any theories as to how it came aboard, Doctor? Contact with the shore authorities, however minimal?'

'I'd doubt that, sir. Dust blown aboard in Port Said, distributed via the ventilators. Flies . . . possibly the fruit and vegetables not washed in disinfectant as thoroughly as they might have been, something missed out.' He shrugged. 'It's very hard to say, but it's not entirely surprising.'

'Well, anyway, it's here now,' Bracewell said. 'We just have to fight it.' He turned to Kemp. 'Do we inform the escort, Commodore?'

Kemp nodded. He made a signal to the flag, for information. When the answering signal was received it contained information of its own: there was cholera aboard the *Glamorgan* and one of the destroyer escorts. Crampton went below again, this time to contact the army's medical section to report a confirmed case. It was just as he reached the boat deck that the sound of the alarm rattlers shattered through the ship and the alleyways became a seething mass of men moving to their boat stations.

EIGHT

'From Captain (D), sir. Am about to attack.'

'Thank you, Lambert.' Kemp focussed his binoculars on the sector of the sea where he would expect to find the feather of water from a periscope. The reports had continued following the first contact; the submarine, nationality still unknown but by this time unlikely to be British, was nearer as a result of the closing courses and was well within torpedo range of the convoy. Kemp had not scattered the ships; but he had ordered the columns farther apart and the distance between ships in column to be extended. The targets were thus more widely dispersed; and the zig-zag was in operation for the first time since leaving the Suez Canal.

Kemp watched the destroyers racing across the flat blue water, crossing to the starboard bow of the right-hand column. He said, 'I wish to God Captain (D) would get on with the attack if he's going to. He's giving the bugger too much time.'

'Maybe the sub'll have gone deep by now, sir.'

'And maybe not, Finnegan.' Kemp was edgy. 'They've not reported lost contact.'

'The Japs have guts, sir. If it's a Jap. I guess I wouldn't like to be in that boat.'

Kemp said nothing. It was true enough about guts. He'd already spoken of a suicide job and that was precisely what it was. That submarine couldn't possibly get away, but in the meantime –

'Torpedo starboard, sir, 090 degrees!' The report came from Lambert, his voice high.

'Captain –'

'All right, Commodore.' Bracewell gave his orders fast. 'Hard a-starboard . . . engines to emergency full ahead!'

The *Orlando* started her swing under full starboard helm so as to present the smallest possible target. Bells rang in the wheelhouse to be repeated back from the starting platform below in the engine-room as Chief Engineer Stouter wrenched his pointers over to follow the indicators on the bridge. A shudder ran through the ship as the increased revolutions bit and the wake began to curve and tumble harder as the ship's head went round to starboard. As the full impact of the helm was felt, the *Orlando* heeled heavily and everywhere men were thrown off their feet, grabbing for support to anything handy. From the galleys and store-rooms, crockery pantries and issue rooms, came the sound of chaos as things flew from their moorings. Chief Steward Bliss shut his eyes and tried not to think about breakages and their effect on his bonus at the end of the voyage when he had to report losses. In the purser's office an unsecured typewriter, one of those with an exceptionally long platen for the typing of port forms, slid from a desk and crashed to the deck. Miss Hardisty, at her boat station along with her girls and a number of men, staggered and found herself willy-nilly in the rough arms of a sergeant, a man of about her own age who grinned at her, called her darling, and slid a hand round her bottom. She was in a state of dither and didn't immediately detach herself from the sergeant's embrace, for which afterwards she mentally kicked herself because the wretched man obviously needed no encouragement. She was still in his embrace when he stepped back suddenly and looked down over the ship's side.

'*Bloody torpedo!*'

The torpedo had passed down the starboard side harmlessly. Simultaneously another was reported passing down the port side. Miss Hardisty felt quite faint; it had been a very close thing indeed. If the ship had been a matter of feet to either side of her avoiding course, they would have been stopped in their tracks by a massive explosion. But faint or not, Rose Hardisty was the PO Wren and immediately she reassured her girls.

'There's no danger,' she said briskly, 'thanks to Captain Bracewell and Commodore Kemp. We're in very good hands.' She straightened her uniform hat, dislodged a little by the sergeant. A moment later the reverberations of exploding depth charges hit the ship as the destroyers at last mounted their attack. Below decks the sound waves through the water clanged and echoed around the ears of the damage control parties and the men standing by the fire hoses along the working alleys and the troop decks. Ex-Colour Sergeant Parkinson heard them with relish. Soon there would be a little less enemy.

'Every little helps,' he remarked to one of the stewards of the hose party.

'Eh?'

'As the old lady said when she piddled in the sea.'

From the bridge Kemp watched the attack through his binoculars. The great spouts of water rose in what seemed to be an unending succession and then a black snout was seen to thrust through the surface like a wounded whale, rising high in the air amid a bubbling of the sea as the tanks continued to blow. Human figures were seen, clinging to the emerging conning tower and the gun mounted on the fore casing, men like flies who, losing their grip as the angle increased, dropped away into the water. As the submarine began quite suddenly to slide back into the deeps, two of the destroyers were seen to race across to pick up survivors. As they went, another signal reached the *Orlando*, this time from Captain (D).

Lambert reported to Kemp. 'No further contacts, sir.'

Finnegan said, 'Hence the ability to pick up survivors, I guess.'

Kemp made no comment. There had been the times, on other convoys as well as this one, when the picking up of survivors, British or enemy, had not been possible. He thought bitterly: for possible read expedient. You didn't put your own men at risk while you were under attack. But it always left that sour taste and a large measure of self blame for leaving men to drown. This time, the submarine's crew had been lucky; they had also been brave. Later that afternoon, it was confirmed that the attacker had indeed been Japanese, a big ocean-going submarine of the *Takatsuki* class.

ii

First Officer Forrest came to the bridge: she came without hesitation now; since that first time before the Malta arrival, when she had been blasted back down the ladder, Kemp had recognized that she came only when essential.

She saluted smartly.

'Yes, Miss Forrest?'

'I've been approached by the ship's surgeon, Commodore. His nursing sister's on the sick list, I'm afraid.'

'I know – Dr Crampton's reported. Cholera . . . we haven't escaped after all. Well, Miss Forrest?'

'Dr Crampton's asked if my Wrens could help out, Commodore.'

'Help out, in what way? You haven't any trained nurses among them.'

'No. Apparently that's not necessary. In the circumstances the girls could – help. Dr Crampton makes the point that all the army orderlies are men, Commodore.'

'I know that. No QAS embarked. I gather that's normal.' Kemp paused, seeing Jean Forrest's embarrassment. 'Yes, yes, I understand.' There would be intimacies to be dealt with, of course. 'Well – it's up to you really. You're their officer.'

'I've no objection, Commodore. The girls want to help. And anyway, we're all in the same boat. Rather literally.'

Kemp gave a bleak smile. 'Yes, true. Volunteers?'

She nodded. 'All of them without exception.'

'So long as that's the case, all well and good.'

Jean Forrest saluted again and turned away down the ladder. She had a feeling that Rose Hardisty had seen to it that all the girls had volunteered. After Dr Crampton had come to see her, she had sent for the PO Wren and put the case to her. Miss Hardisty had said she would talk to the girls; Jean had stressed that they must volunteer and not be conscripted; but Miss Hardisty had a way with her. The first officer had watched her from the start of the convoy when it had left the Clyde, grow into her position of authority and responsibility, and she was very jealous of the good name of her charges. When Miss Hardisty had spoken to her girls Jean Forrest had not been present.

'Now then,' Miss Hardisty had said severely in her old-time role of nanny to a county family. 'You're all going to be needed very badly, relieving each other in looking after that poor sick nurse. It's your duty. Or rather, I'd like you to see it that way. I'd like to see you put self aside. It's a case of you volunteering, of course. I'm taking it you're all going to volunteer. I'm very proud of you all, I must say. You're all a credit to the service, my dears. Yes, Wren Peters?'

'Isn't there a risk –'

'Dr Crampton will be issuing his instructions shortly,' Miss Hardisty said. 'That's all for now.' Wren Peters, she had noted early in the convoy, was not one of the most enthusiastic of her girls, but was easily enough sat on when necessary. There was one more thing Miss Hardisty had to say before she dismissed the muster. 'I shall be taking the first turn of duty myself,' she announced.

iii

Rose Hardisty was, or had been, purely a nursery nurse; by no means a hospital one. But she had nursed her small charges through many a childhood ailment – measles, whooping cough, chicken-pox, even scarlet fever. Always the family doctor had congratulated her afterwards, saying that had it not been for her devoted attentions the story of recovery might have been different. She knew when someone was very ill, knew the moment when crises passed into the first stages of recovery. She knew now, looking down on the sick girl, that Mary McCann was passing towards death. No-one needed to tell her; she knew the signs even though she didn't know cholera. As the troopship steamed on through the Red Sea's

89

terrible heat, still with no air coming down through the ventilators, she sat and sweated at the bedside, face frowning and concentrated, feeling herself all the torments that the racked body was enduring. Mary McCann was growing colder by the minute, it seemed; when Miss Hardisty bent over her, wiping at the face with a damp cloth, the breath itself was strangely cold, almost as though it was passing over an ice-block, and she was suffering badly from the cramps in arms and legs, crying out with the pain. When she tried to speak the voice was low and hoarse.

'Don't talk, dear. Just lie quiet. It'll pass, it'll be better soon. You mark my words.'

Dr Crampton came and went; he couldn't stay long. He whispered to Miss Hardisty, 'More cases, I'm afraid. It's spread faster than I thought likely.'

'The soldiers, Doctor?'

'Yes. The army's had to section off part of the troop deck as an isolation area. Both the padres have gone down with it – C of E and RC. It's not only the army. I've got a number of the ship's crew on the sick list.'

She nodded. 'You've got your hands full, Doctor. Don't worry about Miss McCann, I'll manage.'

'I'm sure you will. I'm very, very grateful. Sister McCann . . . we've sailed together a long while, you know.' Crampton indicated the telephone. 'That'll get me through the exchange. Call me at once, please, if the general condition worsens. I'm hoping she'll fall into a proper sleep, a deep one. If that happens, there's every hope.'

Miss Hardisty knew from his tone that he expected the worst. No sleep came; the girl tossed and turned, complained of the cramps more than ever. She remained clear-headed throughout even though after another spasm she passed into a state of collapse, unable to help herself in any way. When the collapse came, Miss Hardisty rang through for the doctor. There was, she reported, no sign of that deep sleep coming. Crampton came along, shook his head at what he saw. Ten minutes later he rang through to the Master, and Bracewell, after taking the call, climbed slowly from his cabin to the bridge.

'First death, Commodore. Sister McCann. First of many, I suppose.'

iv

The disposal of the body took place that same afternoon; the dead were not kept long in the hot climates of the world. A plank was rigged in the starboard gunport door, the passenger embarkation point in peacetime days. The body, sewn into its canvas shroud, lay beneath the Red Ensign as Bracewell, in the absence of the brigade's padre on the sick list, read the words of the committal.

'Forasmuch as it has pleased Almighty God of His great mercy to take unto himself the soul of our dear sister here departed; we therefore commit her body to the deep . . .'

At the appropriate moment the plank was tilted, there was a movement of the Red Ensign, and the body twisted down into the water as the ship's engines lay briefly stopped. In the engine-room Chief Engineer Stouter awaited the telegraphed order from the officer of the watch on the bridge to set his big, shining shafts into action again to propel the ship on to whatever might await it in the days ahead. Stouter thought of death, of the body that would meander through the depths of the Red Sea until it found rest, of the many bodies that were surely yet to come. Cholera was a scourge and an unkind one in the midst of war, in the midst of so many other forms of death from bombs and torpedoes and gunfire and drowning. As if there wasn't enough to contend with . . . beside him on the starting platform the bridge telegraph rang and the pointers went over to Full Ahead. Stouter saw the power put through, saw the shafts start their spin and felt the shudder of the plates as the screws began their thrust and the ship moved on towards the Gates of Hell.

Bracewell, before going back to the bridge, insisted on Crampton accompanying him to his quarters. Or tried to. 'You were shipmates for a long while, Doctor. You can do with a whisky.'

Crampton shook his head. 'If you'll excuse me, sir. I have a

91

lot to do, so many cases. I'm needed below.' He paused, mopped at the sweat pouring down his face. 'I'm thanking God for those Wrens, more so than ever now. They're splendid.'

'Yes, indeed,' Bracewell said. 'Any more key personnel gone down with it yet?'

'Not from the ship's staff, sir. One of the naval gunners has it, a PO. I'll be having a word with the Commodore.'

Captain Bracewell returned to the bridge. The doctor went below to carry on. Petty Officer Ramm watched him go and believed himself struck by a miracle insofar as it wasn't him who was needing medical attention to date. It had after all been Perryman who'd succumbed, which was in a way natural seeing what his gut was like. Ramm's diarrhoea and sickness had cleared up. In his ditty box he'd found a bottle of Dr J. Collis Browne's Chlorodyne, stowed there by his wife back in Pompey and forgotten about till now. That had done the trick, cured what must have been simple gyppo tummy.

He'd been lucky. But the bottle of cure-all had the effect of reminding him of his wife and the proximity to her of that barmaid from The Golden Fleece. You never knew; plenty of bombs had fallen on Pompey and could fall again, and Ramm's home and The Golden Fleece were not all that far apart. Civvies got very matey under blitz conditions, swopping yarns in the air-raid shelters, gossiping while they knitted. Things could come out.

Best forget about it, Ramm told himself. He went aft along the boat deck, towards the 6-inch in the stern. There was another bit of luck to concentrate on: sorry as he was about PO Perryman, his removal from the scene did leave himself back in full charge of his own ratings, and Perryman's as well. Of course, he hoped poor old Perryman would recover; but if he didn't, well. And if he did, he'd be far too shaky on his feet to act the senior gunner's mate this side of Trinco.

Ramm had words with the after gun's crew, finding fault like any PO. That way, you kept the lads up to the mark. Ramm was lucky in finding a small patch of rust on the breech-block. He made the most of that.

There were no more gins in Kemp's cabin now; Jean Forrest was too busy. With all the girls helping out still with the escalating case-load, Jean acted as relief where and when required, letting the girls get away for meal breaks and to catch up on their sleep. The result was that she got no sleep herself and after some forty-eight hours was feeling the strain.

Miss Hardisty remarked on this. 'You're overdoing it, ma'am.'

'Oh no, I'm fine.'

'Beg pardon, ma'am, but you're not.' Great hollows under the eyes, haggard cheeks and a twitch at the corner of the mouth didn't add up to being fine. Miss Hardisty went on, 'I'll take myself off the rota, ma'am, and take watch-and-watch with you for the reliefs. That'll spread it a little, ma'am, and we've got to be sensible.'

Jean, too tired to argue, merely nodded. Miss Hardisty went on a bit more, talking about it being risky to lower one's resistance against the cholera. It would never do, she said, for Miss Forrest to go down with it; she clucked like a mother hen.

That afternoon, Jean Forrest collapsed whilst walking along an alleyway beneath what had been the first-class lounge. She was picked up by Chief Steward Bliss.

'Oh, dearie me,' he said. 'Poor lady.' He was joined by one of the army staff from the orderly room: RSM Pollock, who took over the burden, lifting Jean Forrest in his arms like a baby.

'Cabin,' he said briefly. 'Where is it, Mr Bliss?'

'I'll show you, Sar'nt-Major.'

'Right you are, then. Call the doctor, eh?'

'I'll see to that,' Bliss said.

The WRNS officer was laid gently on her bunk and RSM Pollock stood back. She looked in a bad way, face white and lifeless, totally unconscious with it. Might be the cholera, probably was. RSM Pollock waited until the doctor came, then went along to his own cabin for a quick wash. You had to be careful even though the medics said you couldn't catch the cholera by simple contact. Then he returned to the orderly room. Two of the staff had gone down with the cholera and their replacements were as thick as planks, which put a good deal more strain on RSM Pollock. And there was much to do: the ship was due off the port of Aden in two days' time and a number of decisions had to be made before then. Decisions of that sort were not the RSM's province but the carrying out of the subsequent orders would be.

On entry to the orderly room, Pollock looked around. 'Where's Captain Archer?' he asked.

'Latrine, Sar'nt-Major.'

'Shits, eh. Not too good.' Pollock thought to himself, I reckon we'll get along without him.

vi

The conference was called in the Master's day cabin. Kemp was present, with OC Troops, the battalion commanders, the senior medical officer and Mr Pollock, together with Purser Rhys-Jones, Dr Crampton and the chief steward. On the agenda was the advisability of entering Aden, which had not been on the original routeing instructions from the War Office or the Naval Control on the Clyde.

Kemp started the ball rolling. 'We'll have to lie off under the quarantine flag at all events, just to embark cholera vaccine. If they can supply, that is. Now: does medical opinion support the idea of landing the worst cases?'

The lieutenant-colonel RAMC answered that, after a glance at Crampton. 'Frankly, no. I doubt if they'd take them anyway. And they'd be no better off in my opinion. Aden's a hell-hole if ever there was one. We can cope.'

Bracewell said, 'It would relieve the strain, Colonel.'

'I said we can cope, and we can. I don't like the idea of landing my problems. It's not as though it's a case of something outside the ship's ability. Such as a major operation for which I might not have the specialists.'

A cough came from OC Troops. Pumphrey-Hatton was lying back in his chair, eyes closed, finger-tips together in a position reminiscent of a parson. He said, 'There will be no landings at Aden, gentlemen. None at all.'

The RAMC officer shrugged. Kemp said, 'I beg your pardon, Brigadier?'

Pumphrey-Hatton didn't respond directly. He disregarded Kemp and spoke to Bracewell. 'If the ship should enter Aden, or simply lie off, then the same orders apply as at Alexandria and Port Said.'

There was a brief silence. Kemp broke it, sharply. 'To which orders do you refer, Brigadier?'

Pumphrey-Hatton looked at him then – stared superciliously with raised eyebrows. 'Obvious, I'd have thought. The orders about the men being confined below decks until the ship leaves.'

A small tic started up in Kemp's cheek and his face darkened angrily. 'In Aden of all places? With cholera rife?'

'Confinement makes no difference to the cholera.'

'It makes a lot of difference to the men. What are your reasons, Brigadier?'

'The same as before. There will be enemy agents in Aden. So the same considerations apply.'

'What damned nonsense!' Kemp burst out.

OC Troops sat up straighter, eyes glinting now. 'It's not up to you, Commodore, to criticize the War Office or myself. Full secrecy was and is the order. If this ship enters Aden, then the troops will be confined below decks and that is final.'

Kemp said, 'On the contrary. It is far from final. The men will *not* be confined below decks. It is my decision as Commodore whether or not the ship detaches into Aden from the convoy and then overtakes after – if I decide to enter, then it will not be at the expense of the physical discomfort of the troops.'

Pumphrey-Hatton began to splutter. Moisture ran from one corner of his mouth. 'You have no damn jurisdiction over –'

'As Commodore I have, for certain purposes which do not of course include any usurping of the Master's authority, full jurisdiction for the convoy and those taking passage in it –'

'Damn you, I –'

'And I consider the order for confinement to be plainly and

95

simply idiotic and inhuman and it will not be given. I shall remind you, Brigadier, of another fact of service life. As a commodore RNR I rank with you as a brigadier. But as a naval officer of equivalent status, I in fact outrank you or any other officer of brigadier's rank. You will therefore obey *my* orders – not I yours. I trust that is quite clear.'

This time the silence was longer. Kemp felt remarkably pompous. He had always detested any suggestion of pulling rank. But this time he was determined to stop Pumphrey-Hatton in his tracks and he meant to stick to his guns come what may.

NINE

Now it was war; war of a different sort from the fight against the Axis powers and the cholera. War between the Convoy Commodore and the Officer Commanding Troops was very much to be regretted, but Kemp felt that it had been none of his making. He considered Pumphrey-Hatton's attitude to be wholly unreasonable, and, as he had said in so many words, inhuman. It was said that there was a particular kind of army officer who was impervious to reason; Kemp believed that he had come up against such a one.

Pumphrey-Hatton had got to his feet and stalked jerkily out of the Captain's day cabin without more ado. The battalion commanders had got to their feet, looking somewhat uncertain and, half apologetically, had followed their lord and master. The RAMC colonel, Dr Munro, had remained.

He said, 'I'm with you, Commodore.'

'I'm glad someone is.'

Munro laughed. 'I fancy all the men will be! It's damnable. I've had words with the brigadier already, pointed out that health's as vital as secrecy. More so, in this idiotic situation. He's got a bee in his bonnet about it. I don't like . . .' Munro hesitated, glanced sharply at RSM Pollock whose face remained expressionless. He changed the subject. 'I just hope Aden will let us have that vaccine. I suppose there's no chance of asking ahead?'

'We don't break wireless silence at sea, Colonel.'

'No, quite. I was just thinking . . . that Jap submarine.

97

Won't she have reported our presence, the presence of the convoy? In which case –'

Kemp broke in. 'I doubt if she'll have reported anything. She was submerged on first contact by the destroyer screen, and she surfaced only very briefly. I doubt if they'll have got any messages away, even if their W/T was working after the depth charge attack.'

Munro shrugged. 'Oh, well. I don't suppose it would make much difference anyway. If they've got the stuff, they'll let us have it. If they've enough, that is. They have their own garrison to think about, of course.'

Munro excused himself; like Crampton, who left the Captain's quarters with him, he had much to do amongst the sick. A discussion with Bracewell, the purser and chief steward followed; if Kemp made the decision to enter, stores would be embarked – fresh fruit and vegetables from an area that could be presumed free of the cholera. The chief engineer had not been called to the conference, at his own request: he was needed below where there was a slight difficulty in the engine-room. In any case, his concern was only with his oil fuel supply, and the bunkers had been topped up in Port Said, all the ships refuelling from Royal Fleet Auxiliary tankers, since Aden, the usual bunkering port, had not then been on the list of calls.

When the conference ended Kemp rang down to the ship's surgery and spoke to Dr Crampton. 'Miss Forrest,' he asked. 'How is she now, Doctor?'

'Not too good, I'm afraid –'

'Cholera?'

'Yes, I'm afraid so. I've just this minute confirmed it.'

'Can I see her?'

'No reason why not, sir, I suppose.'

'You sound doubtful.'

'Do I? I'm not really. It's just that . . . well, she looks very sick. You may get a shock.'

'I'm well inured to shocks,' Kemp said. 'I'll be down.'

He hung the handset back on its hook. Jean Forrest, always smart. Very attractive, as he had begun to notice. Reliable, conscientious – all the virtues in his book. It was a damned shame that she should go down with such a filthy disease –

but then she was just one of many. It was the fact that she had been under no operational compulsion to be here at all that stuck in the throat. You didn't get cholera in Britain these days and she'd had no need to leave Britain's shores if she hadn't volunteered for the draft for those personal reasons connected with another brigadier . . .

Kemp caught himself up: he was becoming allergic to brigadiers and that would never do.

He went below.

ii

RSM Pollock was talking to his opposite number – Mr Privett, Regimental Quarter Master Sergeant on the orderly room staff. The subject was the conference. RQMS Privett, who had not been present, was told about the intervention of the Commodore.

'I reckon he was right, Mr Pollock.'

'So do I, Mr Privett. So do I. But it's put the brigadier in a nasty frame of mind, that it has.'

'A wounded tiger.'

'Eh? Well, yes, in a sense.'

'Dangerous, Mr Pollock. We'd best all watch our step for a while.' RQMS Privett twirled at his moustache. Privett was on the elderly side, recalled to the Colours from pension back in '39. In his day, the sergeant-major and the RQMS had more often than not waxed their moustaches, and so Mr Privett did now. The truth was that the Red Sea's heat wasn't good for wax, and Mr Privett looked remarkably like a sad-faced walrus. 'God can be, well, vindictive.'

RSM Pollock said, 'It's not for us to criticize, Mr Privett. Not senior officers.'

'No, course not.'

Suddenly Pollock laughed. 'God, you said. That's just the trouble. He's been broke to the ranks. God's on the bridge now. Convoy Commodore. God the Father. And Captain Bracewell, God the Son.' He paused. 'Mind, that's not criticism.'

'Course not.' The RQMS frowned and twirled again at his sagging moustache. 'I've been thinking. Thought a lot the last few days. The brigadier's been . . . well, very tetchy like. Jumpy. Bag o' nerves, I'd say.' He paused. 'I've heard talk. Talk about some fly-blows in his gin . . .'

'Yes, I heard it too. Take no notice, Mr Privett, that's my advice.' Pollock looked hard at the RQMS. 'Are you suggesting something else, by any chance?'

'Well . . . no. Not really. The strain o' war –'

RSM Pollock became official. 'Careless talk, Mr Privett. I warn you not to repeat it. There's nothing wrong with the brigadier. He's had a hard war, like the rest of us. Some more than others. Get me?'

RSM Pollock turned away, marched smartly along the deck with his cane beneath his left arm. A hard war was what he happened to know Pumphrey-Hatton had had. Not only in this lot. In the 1914–18 war, the brigadier had been a subaltern with his regiment, the Duke of Cornwall's Light Infantry from Bodmin. Pumphrey-Hatton's battalion had been cut to ribbons in the first of the big battles on the Western Front, and Pumphrey-Hatton had been severely wounded, out of action for months, then back again to the horrors, the mud and slaughter in France. In this war he'd got out from Dunkirk by the skin of his teeth, wounded again whilst helping with the embarkation of the troops into the rescue fleet from the south coast of England. He'd earned a mention in despatches from the Commander-in-Chief, General Lord Gort. Later, in the Western Desert – in Tobruk, on attachment to General Sir Leslie Morshead's Australian Division, he'd won a DSO. And his only son had been killed in an air raid over London. At the same time, so had his wife. All this, RSM Pollock had heard from Pumphrey-Hatton's batman, who'd been with him since the days of peace. Pumphrey-Hatton was no Whitehall Warrior with rolled umbrella and bowler hat. Which, come to think of it, was why he, Pollock, was disturbed by what the RQMS had hinted at. The truth was, the brigadier was starting to behave like one of those pea-minded bastards from the safety of the bunkers beneath the offices of state.

Pollock went on his way below, thinking of the curious

100

degrees of God as manifested in the armed forces of the Crown. He himself was God to the troops; he had his God too – his colonel. Colonels had Gods – the General Staff, whose own God was ultimately the Monarch himself by way of the Secretary of State and the Prime Minister. There were classes of God – First, Second and Third. But, as Pumphrey-Hatton was in the process of discovering for himself, the only God that counted while they were aboard a ship was the God on the bridge.

iii

Jean Forrest was pale and shivering, unable to keep still as she lay on the bunk. Also, she was weepy, so much so that she could scarcely speak.

Kemp was out of his element, had no idea what to say, how to offer comfort. He reached out and put a hand on her shoulder and murmured something totally inadequate about feeling better soon. Miss Hardisty, at his side and looking desperately unhappy, did the talking for him, stating the obvious.

'The Commodore's come to see you, ma'am.'

She nodded without speaking, her eyes, large and luminous, on Kemp.

'I've told him you'll be right as rain soon, ma'am.' Miss Hardisty glanced up at Kemp. His large frame seemed to fill the small cabin. 'He says you're not to worry about anything, ma'am, not for now. Once you're up, you'll see all the girls are being looked after, isn't that right, sir?'

'Quite right, Miss Hardisty. Just get better, Miss Forrest. That's all that's required of you.'

She looked at him again and there was a flash of humour in her eyes. 'King's Regulations for sick WRNS officers, Commodore?'

'That's it exactly.'

Her body seemed to jerk and suddenly, surprisingly, she said, 'God save the King, then. I mean that. I'd like to see him victorious. But I won't. I'm going to die. I know that.'

Kemp was shocked. He said sharply, 'Nonsense. Please don't talk like that.'

'I'm sorry,' she said. It was little more than a whisper. She closed her eyes and seemed to sag, to droop in the bed though she went on shivering. Kemp caught the PO Wren's eye and moved away. She left the cabin with him.

'Poor lady,' she said. 'She's been overdoing it, sir. That won't help. The resistance, you see, sir, it's lowered.'

Kemp nodded. When he turned away to go back to the bridge, there were tears in his eyes. He hoped the PO Wren hadn't seen that. A weeping commodore wouldn't inspire much confidence in anybody.

iv

Pumphrey-Hatton was in his stateroom, chain smoking, trembling with anger. He'd always regarded the Navy with suspicion: they thought they knew it all and they were so damned superior in their attitude, so conscious of being the Senior Service, aided and abetted in this attitude, this certainty, by the King himself. His Majesty didn't discriminate, of course, but it was a well-known fact that he preferred to wear naval uniform rather than anything else, and also he'd served in the fleet from midshipman to lieutenant himself. There was bound to be a bias. This was a disloyal thought, and Pumphrey-Hatton thrust it from his mind.

This Aden business – that was what he had to concentrate on.

Should he give the order?

He had said in no uncertain terms that he intended to. He could scarcely back down with any dignity. On the other hand, the order given, that oaf on the bridge would countermand it. What, then, would be his position as OC Troops? He would be a laughing-stock to his own officers and men. The effect on discipline would be appalling.

The stick he was in was a very cleft one indeed.

Pumphrey-Hatton lifted his gin glass with a shaking hand, spilling some on the carpet left from the opulence of peace. No fly-blows now: he had dealt with slackness firmly. But as a precaution he examined the glass carefully each time. By now the flies had largely departed, but quite a few had been left below decks when the ship had cleared from the confines of the Gulf of Suez, and these could be very dangerous. He had got the RAMC to spray his stateroom, bedroom and bathroom with something that they had assured him would kill flies but this hadn't been entirely successful. Some flies as it were broke through the defences. Like the Hun at Tobruk . . .

There was no security, none.

Pumphrey-Hatton called for his batman, Private Oliver.

'Yessir?'

'Oliver, my compliments to Colonel Munro. He's to send up anything he's got on flies and diseases pertaining thereto. At once.'

'Yessir.' Oliver hesitated. 'Flies, sir?'

'That's what I said, man, or are you deaf?' Pumphrey-Hatton was shouting now.

'Nossir – yessir! At once, sir.' Private Oliver turned about; boots failed to thud on carpets but the motion was very parade-ground. When the man had gone on his errand, Pumphrey-Hatton walked up and down the stateroom, looking from the square ports at the sunlit blue of the Red Sea, shimmering like an electric fire's reflection from a chrome backing. A terrible place; Pumphrey-Hatton scratched at his chest. There was a very worrying itch, like eczema. Of course, it was only prickly heat – he knew that. Have a shower and it would go. But there was no shower now. The showers were fresh water, which was scarce and had been since Alexandria. He could have a salt-water bath but that left one sticky, and that made the prickly heat worse.

It was damn *ridiculous* that OC Troops couldn't get rid of his prickly heat! When his batman came back with some sort of treatise on flies, Pumphrey-Hatton threw it bad-temperedly onto a table and demanded to see the ship's purser.

'What are you going to do about OC Troops?' Bracewell asked as he stood with Kemp in the bridge wing. Once through the Gates of Hell the decision had been taken to enter Aden, go to the anchorage and request vaccine and stores. The signals had been exchanged with the Flag; the *Orlando* would detach from the convoy at dusk the following day. Since the call was to be a short one, it had been decided that the rest of the convoy and its escort would remain outside the port rather than allow the big troopship to follow on behind like an arse-end Charlie on an overtaking manoeuvre. While the Commodore was in the port, the ships would maintain their steaming speed up and down with the asdics fully operational and the destroyer screen on the alert.

Kemp answered Bracewell's question. 'I'm not going to do anything about him. It's up to him.'

'But if he gives the order?'

'I don't believe he will, Captain.'

'I can only hope not.' Bracewell was a shade diffident. He went on, 'It's put me in a somewhat equivocal position as a matter of fact.'

'Yes, and I'm sorry. You're the Master – I know.'

'I'm not sure it isn't my prerogative, strictly. As you know, I've not sailed with a commodore before. It's a new and somewhat uncertain position for me. Those troops – they're my passengers in a sense.'

'A very positive sense. Perhaps – I've been thinking about this – I said too much. Overstepped myself. Yet what I said remains what I feel. We can't have the troops subjected to stupid whims and fancies. The secrecy angle's tripe and we all know it.'

'Yes. Oh, I agree, but –'

'Are you with me on this, Bracewell?' Kemp asked directly, turning to face the Master.

Bracewell nodded. 'Yes . . . yes, I am. You have my assurance – I shall back you. But, frankly, I'd rather not. I think you understand, Commodore?'

Kemp did, having been a liner's master himself. He

understood only too well. Brigadiers could make a good deal of noise after the event. Whitehall could take note, and probably would if the below-decks confinement order had come from there, which in fact Kemp believed it might not have done – it might have been the personal idea of oc Troops himself. But if Whitehall had indeed been the originators, then there could be frosty communication with Bracewell's owners in the City and next time home Bracewell would be called upon to explain. Owners never wanted trouble at any time; now, in war, the trooping contracts were valuable. Not that the War Office, with its great need for transports, would refuse to employ the *Orlando*; but it might well raise objections to a Master who had been party to over-ruling an oc Troops.

Bracewell said, 'I'm wondering if we could find a way out.'

Kemp gave a short laugh. 'I rather doubt that, frankly! If it comes, it's going to be a clash. All or nothing. I can't see any room for a compromise. Can you?'

Bracewell admitted that he couldn't. 'Perhaps oc Troops will have second thoughts. See the light – or something.'

'Well, let's hope so. I don't want any trouble, I assure you. We have troubles enough already.' Kemp paused, searching the sea ahead through his binoculars, one of the almost reflex actions of the war. So often split-seconds counted, that extra time given by spotting the tell-tale feather of water streaming from a periscope, or seeing the dot in the sky that heralded an air attack. His scan completed for the time being, he lowered his binoculars. Coming to a sudden decision he said, 'I'll tell you what. I'll go and have a yarn with Pumphrey-Hatton. Smooth the ruffled feathers!'

Bracewell grinned. 'Apologize, Commodore?'

'If I have to, yes. For being rather too forthright. But I'll stand by what I said. And that's for sure.'

vi

There was the feeling of a death ship now. Below decks, the smell of sweaty bodies and sweat-soaked bedding had given place to medical smells of antiseptic. Carbolic was being freely

105

used, so was permanganate of potassium. When Petty Officer Ramm went below, he felt he was entering hospital which in a sense he was. The spread of the cholera had been fast, unexpectedly so. Of the naval party, four, including PO Perryman, had gone down with it. So far none had died. Of the military draft, there were 310 cases of varying severity and, so far, 47 deaths. The ship's crew was badly depleted; 89 men on the sick list, including three deck officers and one assistant purser. So far the engineers seemed to have escaped. 11 of the deck and catering departments had died; the committal services, Ramm thought, went on for ever and ever. Soon they would run out of canvas for the shrouds, but no doubt a fresh supply would be indented for at Aden.

'Floating coffin,' Ramm remarked, encountering Miss Hardisty.

'What a thing to say, Petty Officer Ramm!'

'True, though.' Ramm sucked at his teeth. 'How's Miss Forrest, eh?'

'Very poorly I'm sorry to say. How's Petty Officer Perryman?'

'Dunno.'

Miss Hardisty was shocked. 'You mean you haven't been to see him, haven't even enquired?'

'Well, I –'

'Commodore Kemp came down to see Miss Forrest. Came down himself, ever so upset he was, and him being on the bridge nearly all the way from home!'

'Well,' Ramm said again. 'I'll look in.' Rose Hardisty said she hoped he would, and went away. Ramm thought that maybe it was his duty; if a commodore could call in on a Wren, then maybe he should do the same for someone of his own branch, and he needn't linger long. And no time like the present, get it over and done with . . . he went along to the ship's surgery and ascertained where Perryman was being treated, in a sort of makeshift ward at the after end of G Deck, hot and stifling and reeking of antiseptic like everywhere else, only more so in the confined spaces so far down in the ship.

They wouldn't let him in; Nightwatchman Parkinson,

106

having had to change his duties on account of the length of the sick list, was on the door.

'Petty Officer Ramm, isn't it? What can I do for you, Mr Ramm?'

'Like to see me mate. Petty Officer Perryman.'

'Perryman, yes. Perryman. Well, the orders are, no-one to enter without due authorization. Got a chit?'

'No, I –'

'Sorry. You can call out to him – he's berthed just inside the door, first bed on the left. Stand in the doorway, all right?'

'All right,' Ramm said, glad enough not to have to go right into an area of infection. 'How is he, eh?'

'Not too bad,' was the answer. 'Else, you wouldn't be allowed conversation.'

Ramm nodded and put his head inside the door. Perryman was reading, a paperback. He looked fairly colourless but that was about all. Ramm called out his name and he looked up.

'You, eh? Nice of you to call.'

'Glad to. How are you?'

'Fair to middling. Quack says I'll recover. Mild case, quack says. Mostly the runs. How's things up top?'

'All on top line. Just one thing.' Ramm couldn't resist it. 'Rust on the breech, 6-inch aft.'

'Not when I was took sick there wasn't,' PO Perryman said promptly. 'Want to watch that, you do. I never did 'ave rust on *my* guns.'

Ramm seethed but kept silent: you didn't exacerbate the sick by arguing the toss. But he would remember that. After another word or two he went away, trying guiltily not to reflect too much on the fact that if Perryman had it only slightly he might well be back to duty before the arrival at Trincomalee. Reading a bloody paperback, Ramm thought, I ask you! He reckoned Perryman was a fraud.

vii

Purser Rhys-Jones had reported as requested to the OC Troops and on returning to his office rang down for the chief steward. 'Mr Bliss – purser here.'

107

'Yes, sir?'

'I have been speaking to oc Troops, Mr Bliss. I have had a most difficult conversation. He insists on having shower facilities restored.'

'The orders, sir –'

'Yes, yes, I know of the orders of course. But it is on account of the prickly heat, you know –'

'Prickly heat, sir? Got it myself. Scratching like a moggy I've been –'

'Yes, yes, but you are not the oc Troops, Mr Bliss, though goodness knows it is not I who would wish to say that there should be exceptions to the order. oc Troops is in a different position, you see, or so he says.' Rhys-Jones wiped sweat from his face and neck and adjusted the electric fan set in the deckhead so that a stream of less hot air wafted over him. 'He is asking to have his shower reconnected, Mr Bliss.'

'That's not possible, sir. It can't be isolated from the rest of the A deck accommodation, and if –'

'Well, yes, I knew that and I said as much but oc Troops still insisted, you see. So we must think of something else. What do you suggest?'

'God knows, sir, I don't.'

'That is not helpful, Mr Bliss.'

No, Bliss thought, it isn't. Why he should be bothered with oc Troops' prickly heat he knew not, but there it was. He said he would think something up and the purser rang off, satisfied that he had passed the buck. Mr Bliss sighed, put away the bundles of paperwork waiting on his desk, and went in search of the chief officer. A conference was held consisting of the chief officer, the senior second engineer, Mr Bliss and his second steward, and the engine-room storekeeper. The problem was attacked and eventually, in the way of seamen accustomed to producing solutions out of thin air, was solved.

viii

There was a knock on the stateroom door.

Pumphrey-Hatton called in a high voice, 'Yes, who is it?'

'Kemp, Brigadier.'

'Really.'

Kemp went straight in; he was not accustomed to being kept waiting outside doors. Pumphrey-Hatton's face was stony. 'What does this mean, Commodore?'

Kemp said, 'There are things we must discuss.'

'Such as?'

'I think you know what I mean, Brigadier. The ship will enter Aden at dusk tomorrow –'

'I'm aware of that, thank you.'

'So there's the question of confinement of the troops.'

'Yes.' Pumphrey-Hatton had not asked Kemp to sit down, but remained seated himself, an overflowing ashtray on a table beside him. 'My order stands. I don't know what you propose to do about it.'

'I suggest you withdraw the order, Brigadier. You must see that it's totally pointless –'

'I do not see that my orders are pointless!' Pumphrey-Hatton got to his feet and stood with his chest heaving and two spots of colour appearing in his cheeks. He faced Kemp like a sparrow confronting a bear. Kemp saw that he had been indiscreet; he offered an apology.

'I don't want your damned apologies, thank you, Kemp.' oc Troops was shaking all over, almost beside himself. 'I'm not going to be treated like some blasted subaltern who doesn't know what he's talking about. I am the Officer Commanding Troops aboard this ship and what I order is my own affair –'

'Not quite, Brigadier. Not entirely. The ship's Master and I –'

'Oh, fiddlesticks! You're simply being obstructive and pandering to the men, playing to the gallery, seeking some sort of damned popularity –'

Kemp, angry himself now, snapped, 'Not so. What do I need popularity for? That's not my job, Brigadier.' He made an effort to restrain his temper and said in a milder tone, 'We have no need to fall out over this. Let me suggest a compromise: we shall enter at dusk and we shall be clear of the port shortly after first light if not before. I –'

'If it's after dark –'

'If it's after dark, which it will be almost on arrival, then the troops won't be seen from the shore. The decks will of course be darkened as will the ports, just the same as at sea. And the troops can if you wish be confined just for the short period of daylight before we're clear away. What cannot be accepted is that they should be confined throughout the night in such conditions as pertain in Aden. Aboard an over-crowded ship prickly heat alone drives men out on deck in the dark hours to find a little cooler air. We can't deny them that, Brigadier.'

Pumphrey-Hatton, his face working and the spots of colour even more pronounced, turned away from Kemp's gaze and began strutting the carpet of his stateroom, fingers balled into fists. He breathed heavily, as though on the verge of a stroke. Big patches of sweat spread from his armpits, staining the khaki-drill tunic. He had swung round and seemed about to address Kemp again when there was another knock on the door. OC Troops seemed glad to be interrupted. He said, 'Yes, who is it?'

'Chief officer, sir. Your shower arrangements.' The door opened and a procession came in: chief officer, purser, second steward, ship's carpenter, a man in oily overalls and two stewards carrying what looked like a tin bath perforated with a number of holes, followed by another steward with a large enamel jug and a deck rating with lathes of thin wood.

'What the devil!'

'It's the best we could do, sir,' the chief officer said. 'We'll rig it up in a jiffy, over your bath. The steward will pour the water. *Fresh* water.'

Pumphrey-Hatton stared. Kemp stared. Then their eyes met; Kemp's look was sardonic, and OC Troops understood very well why. Kemp saw that as well. He left the stateroom, feeling that by a sheer fluke he had made some sort of a point.

TEN

To take the ship into Aden was Captain Bracewell's responsibility but Kemp accorded him the use of his own signal staff, the ship's signalman being on the sick list. Bracewell, as the *Orlando*, now detached from the convoy, made the approach, passed the orders to Yeoman of Signals Lambert.

'Quarantine flag, Yeoman.'

'Yessir. Already bent on, sir.'

'Hoist.'

The yellow quarantine flag was hauled up to the starboard main yardarm. Bracewell said, 'Request permission to enter.'

'Aye, aye, sir.' Lambert flashed the signal to the King's Harbour Master. There was some delay and then the response was signalled. Lambert reported, 'From KHM, sir. Understand you may have cholera aboard.' Lambert interrupted his report to say, 'That'll have been sent ahead by land line or wireless from Port Said, sir.' Bracewell nodded and the yeoman completed the message: 'What is your reason for entering?'

Bracewell said, 'Make, to embark fresh stores and cholera vaccine if available.'

This was flashed across; there was further delay while the ship lay with her engines stopped. The place was airless and oppressive beneath the distant mountains which loomed behind the port. It was dark now. Kemp looked down on the boat deck; troops lined the sides and a buzz of conversation came up on the still air. Pumphrey-Hatton had conceded, the

111

compromise had been reached: that personal shower arrangement, that pulling of rank – it had been very fortuitous and it had done the trick. OC Troops, not speaking again to Kemp, had sent up a note saying that he would reconsider but if there was any come-back then it would be laid at Kemp's own door. Kemp was not worried about come-backs and had sent a soothing note of thanks to OC Troops for his understanding.

That had closed the matter, which Kemp regarded as a storm in a teacup that should never have happened; and he was humble enough to acknowledge that his own forthright attitude had not helped.

After almost half-an-hour of what Kemp irritably regarded as a waste of valuable time, the further signal came from the King's Harbour Master giving permission to enter and indicating anchor bearings in a distant part of the anchorage.

'They're keeping us nicely at bay,' Kemp remarked to Bracewell. 'Understandable, I suppose, but medically unnecessary.'

Bracewell nodded, and passed his orders for getting under way again. As he conned his ship inwards, more signals came, asking for details of store requirements and indicating that a small amount of vaccine would be available. There was a hint that the cholera could spread down from the canal zone and they had their own personnel, naval and military, to consider. KHM asked if any other medical assistance was required. OC Troops had come to the bridge for the entry and was avoiding Kemp's eye, which Kemp considered childish. When Bracewell turned to him in regard to the medical assistance his answer was curt.

'No.'

The ship approached the anchorage, stealing through the darkness of the port, perhaps the most barren and inhospitable harbour of the Empire, a place of burning sun by day, of airless heat and arid ground and more flies. Men swatted at them along the decks, they found their way below to the troop decks and the cabins and in the makeshift sick bays they settled on the sick and the dying. The orderlies of the RAMC, and the Wrens who were still helping out, though in lesser numbers now since four of their number were themselves on the sick list, did what they could to keep the air and the flies moving.

In her cabin, tired to the point of exhaustion now after endless tending of the sick, Miss Hardisty felt a terrible griping pain in her bowels. Soon after this she vomited, and collapsed onto her bunk, feeling like death.

ii

The order to let go the starboard bower anchor went from the bridge to the chief officer standing in the eyes of the ship; there was a roar as the cable, already veered to the waterline, went out, and a cloud of red rust rose above the fo'c'sle-head. With the engines moving slow astern to check her way, the *Orlando* came to her temporary anchorage; the cable was secured with the third shackle on deck. The fo'c'sle party was fallen out once the slips were on, and the engines were rung to stand-by. Bracewell intended to maintain an anchor watch on the bridge, which meant that a stand-by presence would also be required on the starting platform below.

Within a short time a power boat was seen to be coming off from the port. In the interval before it came alongside, Kemp went down to his cabin for a wash and to change into a clean white uniform. He had just entered the cabin when his sound-powered telephone whined.

Wearily he took up the handset. 'Kemp here.'

'Surgery – Crampton, sir. I thought you'd want to know . . . Miss Forrest –'

'Is she –'

'Nothing to worry about, sir. She's come out of the collapse. She's sleeping. That's a very good sign. I have every hope.'

'Thank you, Doctor,' Kemp said. 'Thank you.' He put back the handset and found a shake in his fingers. He felt dizzy, almost light-headed. It had been an enormous relief. He sat down rather violently in his chair and passed a hand over his eyes. Jean Forrest had been much on his mind. As he looked up his gaze lit on the photographs on his desk, three silver

113

frames, Mary his wife, his two seagoing sons, the latter fighting their own destroyer war somewhere in the North Atlantic, escorting the convoys. He looked hard at Mary. Suddenly it came to him that he'd not given her or home a thought since Jean Forrest had been struck down by the cholera.

He was ashamed; he must watch it, must be very careful. But he sent up a prayer, on his knees beside his bunk, giving thanks for a delivery. Then, after his wash and change of uniform, he went along with Finnegan to Bracewell's day cabin. The shore people had been brought up from the starboard gunport door a couple of minutes earlier: KHM in person, an RN captain accompanied by a paymaster lieutenant RNVR, a surgeon commander RN, and two scruffily-clad civilians of Asian aspect who had come in connection with the stores required by the chief steward, to whom they were despatched. OC Troops did not put in an appearance, but the army was represented by one of the battalion commanders and by the senior RAMC officer, Lieutenant-Colonel Munro. There was much discussion about the cholera. The disease had not yet struck Aden and very well might not; the surgeon commander had brought with him such vaccine as he could supply. He confirmed Crampton's already stated view that the vaccine didn't, in fact, confer much immunity but at least it gave a degree of confidence to the layman.

He asked Crampton if he had any special problems. Crampton said he had not. Munro said the same. The disease was simply taking its course and many more would die yet. It was a fact of life, especially under war conditions of over-crowding and poor sanitary arrangements. And suspect foodstuffs. And the ubiquitous flies.

The King's Harbour Master asked Kemp how long he intended staying in the port.

'As short a time as possible, Captain. Just long enough to embark the fresh food. Then we'll be away.'

KHM nodded. 'I understand *Valiant* is joining the escort.'

'That's right. Off Gardafui. Are there any intelligence reports that I should have, movements of the enemy and so on?'

'You've had nothing from Admiralty, no cyphers?'

'None. Total silence.'

'H'm. Well, perhaps the news hasn't yet penetrated, though I'm surprised I must say. We've picked up a report . . . perhaps report's too strong a word, let's say a rumour, that there's a surface raider at large, the *Neuss*. We passed it on a couple of days ago – you should have been informed. Probably some WRNS cypher queen in Whitehall was late for a date –'

'Where is the *Neuss* said to be, Captain?' Kemp broke in.

KHM shrugged. 'Uncertain, but the rumour suggests she's cruising in the northern part of the Indian Ocean. Could be in the Arabian Sea. I can't be precise. Do you know the vital statistics of the *Neuss*, Commodore?'

Kemp was about to say he didn't when Sub-Lieutenant Finnegan took over. 'I guess I do, sir. I've kind of made a study of the raiders –'

'Canadian efficiency,' KHM said. 'Am I right?'

'Not Canadian, sir. American.'

'Ah, so you're one of those who joined the RCNVR. Rare birds, and very welcome. But go on.'

'Yes, sir. *Neuss*, 14,000 tons, carries four 6-inch guns plus ack-ack, two 21-inch torpedo tubes. Maximum speed nineteen knots, cruises at fourteen. Oil fuel capacity means she can stay at sea for four weeks at economical speed. That gives her quite a lot of scope.'

KHM nodded. 'Spot on, sub. Of course, you've got a good cruiser escort. Nothing really to worry about.'

iii

Nothing really to worry about . . .

Kemp thought about the *Valiant*. One of the *Queen Elizabeth* class battleships, laid down before the last war. Of 31,100 tons, those battleships carried eight 15-inch guns in four twin turrets, two for'ard, two aft, plus twelve 6-inch in broadside batteries, four 4-inch AA and close range weapons, two submerged torpedo tubes. They were protected by thirteen inches of armour plate at the waterline and around the heavy gun turrets. The *Valiant*'s speed was problematic. She might manage twenty-two knots with everything but the kitchen sink thrown into the furnaces, but it was unlikely. However, she had the gun power; she would stand and fight with her massive main armament, whatever was encountered.

Kemp, on leaving Bracewell's quarters, went to the bridge where Yeoman of Signals Lambert was busying himself around his flag locker and his signalling projectors.

'*QE* class battleships, Lambert.'

'Yessir?'

'Ever served in them?'

'Not the *QE* class, sir, no. *Resolution*, R class. Very similar, sir. Bit younger, like.'

'What are they like?'

'Like, sir?' Lambert reflected, pushing back his cap to scratch at his head. 'What they *was* like, sir, some years ago now . . . leaky, parts not working at full efficiency, that sort of thing, sir. Hard to keep clean below, rats and cockroaches in the galleys.'

'That's rather what I've heard about them. More so now, I suppose.'

'Very likely, sir. Take the old *Royal Oak* what went down in Scapa back in '39, sir. Said to be almost unseaworthy, leaks everywhere, watertight doors not working, trouble with the shell supply to the turrets, all sorts o' things that shouldn't have been.' Lambert paused. 'You thinking of the *Valiant*, sir?'

'Yes.' No mention yet of the possible proximity of the German raider.

'A bit of a bucket, sir, but she'll be all right. In their way, they're good old ships, sir. Never see the like again, I reckon.'

Kemp smiled to himself: it was just like the British seaman of the lower deck. Moan, but in the end there was nothing like the old days, the old ships. They were less technical and thus more lovable and what they lacked in modern refinements was made up for by the spirit of the ships' companies. The poor old *Valiant* would be all right if the moment came.

Miss Hardisty, possessor of a single-berth cabin since she was the only Wren of her rank aboard, was left in it. There was in any case virtually no space left in the sections of the ship that had been converted into sick quarters. She lay and tossed about, feeling deathly cold, attended by the army's medical orderlies and, for her more private needs, by one of her own WRNS ratings.

She wanted to die, she felt so poorly. She began to have terrible cramps in her legs and arms and stomach. She was violently thirsty, she was restless and became more and more exhausted as the sheer fact of the restlessness took its toll of her strength. Her skin became blue-tinged, her eyeballs seemed sunk in her skull and she developed the *vox cholerica*. Her pulse was weak, her temperature high.

She was aware at one moment that Commodore Kemp was there. Through the pain and the discomfort and a gradual onset of non-awareness, she was yet aware of being paid an honour. Tears came to her eyes at the thought that the Convoy Commodore himself had taken time and trouble to come down and see her.

In that husky voice, she tried to speak. 'You shouldn't have, sir, not really.'

'I wanted to, Miss Hardisty.'

'Oh, sir!'

He said gently, 'Don't talk. Just rest. They're going to get you better. Like Miss Forrest. She's a lot better, so will you be.'

She looked up at him as he bent over the bunk, saw the gleam of gold from the shoulder-straps. Somehow the fact that a very senior officer was taking a personal interest in her helped. She didn't know why; but it did give her the feeling of not being alone, and also the feeling of being perhaps needed so that it was up to her to get back to duty.

Kemp went from Rose Hardisty's cabin direct to the bridge. The fresh food had been brought aboard from lighters and stowed in the chief steward's storerooms. Now it was time to get back to sea and rejoin the waiting convoy. With the bridge personnel at their stations and the engine-room awaiting the first movement order, the anchor was weighed and Bracewell passed the word for slow ahead on the engines. A little before dawn the *Orlando* moved outwards and no-one aboard was sorry to be leaving Aden behind as the convoy and its escort re-formed and continued on passage south for Cape Gardafui and Socotra.

They had barely moved into their columns when Kemp's leading telegraphist came to the bridge to report an urgent cypher received from the Admiralty. This was prefixed Most Secret; and it was passed to Finnegan, one of whose duties was the decyphering of such signals. When broken down the signal, as Kemp had already suspected, confirmed the report from the King's Harbour Master: the *Neuss* was out, and was believed to have moved north into the Arabian Sea.

'So we could meet her between Gardafui and Colombo, sir.'

Kemp grunted impatiently. 'Where else, Finnegan, since that's the way we're going.'

'Sorry, sir.' Finnegan paused. 'The signal doesn't say . . . I wonder if the *Neuss* has got word of the convoy? And that we have troops aboard.'

'Don't let oc Troops hear your prognosis, Finnegan!'

'You mean the uniforms could have been spotted in Port Said or Suez, sir?'

'Unlikely,' Kemp said. 'The confinement order was obeyed to the full. But I've an idea I'm in for a session of I-told-you-so.'

'I guess you're right, sir,' Finnegan said sympathetically. 'That stuffed –'

'All right, Finnegan. That signal – it was addressed to the Flag in the first place –'

'Repeated Commodore and Captain (D), sir, yes.'

'And the other ships of the escort will be informed by light.' Kemp paused, looking back across the night-dark waters towards the receding rocks of Aden. 'I'll have to pass it to the troops. They have to know the score. But first, there's that brigadier.'

He went down the ladder to the Master's deck and on towards Pumphrey-Hatton's stateroom.

During the forenoon Kemp broadcast to the whole ship over the tannoy, putting them all in the picture as he liked always to do. Captain Bracewell had agreed, as had Pumphrey-Hatton. oc Troops had surprised Kemp, who had expected an ear-bashing about who knew best in regard to the confinement of uniformed soldiers. But Pumphrey-Hatton had taken the news calmly, had just seemed happy to have been vindicated; he agreed with Kemp that it was unlikely any troops had been seen in the circumstances and left it at that. Word of the convoy could have leaked from many other sources; Hitler had plenty of listening ears throughout the Mediterranean and the Middle East.

After the broadcast, rsm Pollock marched along the boat deck and halted alongside Petty Officer Ramm who was checking the close range weapons mounted at the after end.

'Good morning, po. Now – what about this *Neuss*. Know anything about her, do you?'

'Not personally. Never heard of her to tell the truth, Sar'nt-Major.'

'Ha. Got heavy guns, the Commodore said.'

'Yes. No heavier than our 6-inch, o' course. But they'll shoot better.'

'How's that, then?'

Ramm laughed cynically. 'Cos they're a sight younger, that's how. Ours, they're bloody obsolete, in their second childhood. Dug out from a scrapped cruiser of the last war. Best they could do – all the dems-equipped merchant ships have the same sort of thing.'

'H'm.' rsm Pollock rocked backwards and forwards on the balls of his feet. 'What are the chances do you suppose, po?'

'Chances of what? Sinking her? She won't have it all her own way, what with our cruisers and destroyers. We got more total gun-power. I'm not worried about no *Neuss*.'

'I meant, chances of meeting her.'

Ramm said, 'Dunno. Sea's a big enough place, Sar'nt-Major. Needle in a haystack, could be. Like I said, I'm not worried. All the time you're at sea, you take the risk. Not like the pongoes if I may say so without offence. When you're not in action, you're somewhere nice and safe.'

RSM Pollock stiffened and went red. 'Don't talk bloody daft,' he said, and marched away. The very way he moved showed the offence, showed that he was thinking the Navy took things too lightly. Ramm lifted two fingers behind the retreating ramrod back. Ramm had one thought uppermost in his mind: if they did happen to meet the *Neuss*, and if Perryman wasn't yet back to duty, he would be in charge of the guns. His moment of glory might come. He thought about heroes from the recent past, Captain Kennedy of the armed merchant cruiser *Rawalpindi*, Captain Fogarty Fegen of the *Jervis Bay*. He thought of the gunnery rates who had kept their guns in action in both those outgunned ships and he reflected that maybe he would one day be spoken of in the same breath, even though the simile was not exact – these old ex-liners had been operating on their own, no escort. Poor old Perryman, he'd give his eye teeth for the chance, but it looked like being one up for Pompey over Chatham.

The convoy continued southwards. In the morning watch next day under a brilliant sunrise, they were off Cape Gardafui. Upon an exchange of signals between the flagship and the Commodore after clearing Socotra, the course of the convoy was altered to the south-east for the passage diagonally across the Arabian Sea for the southern tip of Ceylon.

Just before six bells in the forenoon watch, Yeoman Lambert reported a ship hull down on the starboard bow.

'Looks like a destroyer, sir. Another coming up now, sir.'

It was almost certainly the *Valiant*'s escort, Kemp believed. Just the same, he saw Bracewell's hand hover over the action alarm. At sea in war, you took no chances. Then there was a winking light and Lambert reported the day's identification being made.

'Acknowledge,' Kemp said. Lambert made the response. They waited, knowing that this was not the enemy. Five minutes later Lambert reported topmasts astern of the destroyer escort, with fighting-tops. Slowly, the old *Valiant* came into view. Cheering rose from the crowded decks and rang out across the shimmer of the water towards the battleship and her big guns. They were going to be all right now, if they hadn't been before.

ELEVEN

The *Valiant*, under a captain's command, did not take over as senior ship of the escort. The rear-admiral commanding the cruiser squadron remained as senior officer, with the *Valiant* giving independent support with her own destroyer escort. The joining ships took station astern of the convoy and a number of signals were exchanged. *Valiant* it appeared had no knowledge of the current movements of the *Neuss*.

Kemp was conferring with Captain Bracewell when OC Troops came up the ladder. He gave Kemp a stiff nod; there was still the underlying friction.

'Good morning, Captain. The sick list – I've just had it from the orderly room.'

'Bad?'

Pumphrey-Hatton thrust the piece of paper into Bracewell's hand. 'Read for yourself.'

Bracewell did, then passed the list to the Commodore. 73 new cases, just over 100 passed through the worst patch and expected to recover. 18 more deaths, one of them Captain Archer. Kemp remarked on that.

'Oh, Archer, yes.' OC Troops was indifferent. 'I dare say somebody will miss him. What's bad is my sar'nt-major. Sick, very.'

Kemp, somewhat shaken at the brigadier's summary dismissal of Captain Archer, looked down again at the list and saw the name, Pollock. He failed to see that stalwart figure laid low, unable to help himself, being treated like a baby,

122

vomiting his heart out. Pollock would take it very badly indeed so long as he was conscious of what was going on.

'Burials,' Pumphrey-Hatton said briskly. 'Same routine, I take it, Captain?'

'No change,' Bracewell answered. The sea committals took place daily during the afternoon watch, the engines being stopped while the gruesome business was carried through, one corpse after another flopping formlessly down into the water, all ranks together, and both sexes too: three of the WRNS ratings had died whilst on passage of the Red Sea before the Strait of Bab el Mandeb and the Aden entry. Kemp had made a point of being present each day, standing at the salute as the planks were tilted and the bodies vanished. He had been particularly saddened by the girls' deaths. After one such heart-rending occasion he had gone below to see Jean Forrest, who was on the recovery list after her long, refreshing sleep following the state of collapse that at the time had seemed so final.

'I hate it,' he said in reference to the committals. 'No families there.'

'It's the same for all.'

'Yes. But I've always thought . . . well, with young girls it's different.'

She gave a thin smile. 'You're an idealist, Commodore. You don't see women as part of any war. But remember Boadicea. She was a warrior queen, wasn't she?'

'She was, but for her own vanity and glorification I dare say. There's a difference. However, we'll not go on about it – just put me down as an old fuddy-duddy who likes to think of himself as a father figure.'

She gave a quiet laugh at that and said, 'You don't do yourself justice, Commodore Kemp.'

He lifted an eyebrow. 'Oh? How's that?'

'Oh, nothing really,' she said, smiling. She didn't pursue the subject and neither did Kemp, but long after he'd left the cabin he was thinking about the look she'd given him from behind her smile.

Along with the fresh stores, the port authorities at Aden had provided canvas already cut into shroud lengths: modern liners didn't carry sailmakers with their sailmakers' palms and horny, deft fingers. But among her crew was an old-time able seaman who had done his time in the sailing ships like both Kemp and Bracewell. Able Seaman Brownlow was an old man by seafaring standards, 65-plus and should have been due for retirement not long after the outbreak of war; but there was that war on, and anyway Brownlow didn't hanker much after the shore. He'd never married and he had no relatives left now. The sea was his life, the *Orlando* had been his home for many years past; as each set of Articles expired and the crew was paid off by the purser in the presence of a deck officer, a Ministry of War Transport official and the local representative of the National Union of Seamen, old Brownlow always automatically signed on again when the new set of Articles was opened.

He was always wanted, because he was a good hand, reliable and conscientious, a seaman to his fingertips but one who had never wanted to rise to the rank of bosun or even bosun's mate. He was an individualist and preferred a quiet life without responsibility over others. He knew his place in the scheme of things, knew he wasn't cut out for command however lowly the capacity. But he was a mine of information on many things, notably on how things were done in the old days, in the old way of the seaman. And after Aden, though he was no qualified sailmaker, it was to him that the ship's bosun came for advice on the lengths of canvas sent aboard from the shore.

'Not like the last lot, Brownie.'

'Eh? What's the difference, then?' It had fallen to Brownlow to complete the home-produced shrouds after Suez, after the first deaths; he did the sewing up, in the traditional way, with the last stitch through the nose of the corpse, the idea being that in the old days, with no doctor embarked, the fact of death was at times uncertain and in theory at any rate the needle through the nose would bring the not really dead to life double quick before it was too late. He had enough sailmaking knowledge for that; when sails had been storm-ripped on passage of Cape Horn, say, it had been a case of all hands to the assistance of the sailmaker himself.

'Too ruddy short, some of them,' the bosun said. 'Take a look, Brownie, see what you can do.'

'Stitch two lengths together, I reckon, if they're that short.'

'Right, I'll leave it to you, then.' The bosun hesitated. 'Got to look ahead. I keep an eye lifting on the sick list, the really bad ones, in the orderly room. That big bloke, the sergeant-major. He's bad.'

Brownlow sucked in his cheeks; he had few teeth and the indrawn cheeks gave him a skull-like aspect. 'Six-foot plus, and big with it. I'll get a big 'un ready. Mind, I reckon they do shrink with the cholera. All that vomiting, and the diarrhoea.'

Unaware of the preparations being made for his disposal, RSM Pollock lay in the cabin which, like PO Wren Hardisty, he had to himself. His breathing was hard and his face had fallen in and the terrible cramps were racking his body, which felt as cold as ice. The diarrhoea and the vomiting had left him as weak as a kitten physically, but his mind was crystal clear and now it was going home across the long sea distances to his home in Carlisle. He was seeing Louise his wife as clear as if she were alongside his bunk; he saw his children, four of them, three boys and a girl, all in their teens and the boys, when last he'd been home, raring to join the war and follow in his footsteps, almost praying that it wouldn't end before they could join up. He'd told them not to be so daft, war was no ruddy picnic, not like peace-time soldiering and even in peace-time until you became at least a corporal, soldiering could be a kind of hell under some NCOs.

Not that there had been many bad ones in his regiment, which was The Border Regiment. His home regiment, with its depot in Carlisle Castle itself. Lying in his bunk, drained and knowing he was close to death, he saw himself when for the first time, dressed in civvies, he'd made his way across the drawbridge, under the arch and onto the parade ground between St Mary's Tower and the barrack blocks, to report for

125

recruit training. He'd been very raw, though no more so than the other lads; and over the next months he'd come to know that parade ground too well, marching, doubling, forming fours, handling a rifle, fixing bayonets, stared at and criticized by drill sergeants, the sar'nt-major, the company officers. How they'd all detested that sar'nt-major until they came to realize he was more, much more than a loud voice and a Sam Browne belt across an ample stomach.

Passing-out as a Trained Soldier under the eye of the Colonel had been a red-letter day in Private Pollock's early life. He'd taken to it all like a duck to water and in no time had had his first stripe as a lance-jack. Then pretty quickly to corporal and the pride of standing out from the rank-and-file when the battalion had marched through the town, admired by the civvies, behind the fifes and drums playing *D'ye ken John Peel*.

There had been training periods among the Cumberland fells when the battalion had marched, again behind the fifes and drums, out from the town through Brampton and along by Hadrian's Wall into the wild country . . . days often enough of hardship in the wintry weather, pleasant days in the summer season, all days that had helped to make men of young soldiers. Then there had come overseas drafts when young Corporal Pollock was attached to the foreign service battalion. Trooping to Bermuda, Gibraltar, India . . . home on early relief from India after a bad go of blood poisoning following a wound sustained on the North-West Frontier, home as a full-blown sergeant, promoted young, to marry a local girl – her old man had been a respected butcher in Carlisle and was always on at Bill Pollock to chuck the army and go into his business, which was a flourishing one, but Sergeant Pollock's life was the army, or more specifically the regiment. He had been determined to end up as RSM, the Colonel's right-hand man, the very embodiment of the regiment and the regiment's pride.

And all for this?

RSM Pollock groaned aloud: the pain of the cramps, the sickness, was almost more than a man could bear, but bear it he must and would. It might not be for much longer.

He was aware of persons in his cabin, looking down at him.

126

Two men, seamen he fancied. One with a peaked cap and a badge, the other an old man in a white singlet and blue trousers. They were examining him, but they certainly were not medics. They muttered and nodded and then someone else entered. RSM Pollock made an attempt to straighten his limbs, hearing the brisk voice of OC Troops.

'You two. Who the hell are you?'

'Bosun, sir, and –'

'What do you want with my sar'nt-major?'

The answer came clear as if the sick man had cloth ears or was too far gone to hear. 'Measuring up, sir. Question of the –'

'Get out.'

'But –'

'Get out!' Pumphrey-Hatton was shouting. 'Get out at once, damn you!'

When the two had gone, OC Troops, simmering down, spoke to the RSM. 'Well, Pollock. Very sorry to see you like this. How are you?'

Pollock made a big effort. 'Not . . . too bad, sir.'

'H'm. Well, I'm glad to hear you say that. Very glad. I'll be gladder still to see you back to duty. With Captain Archer gone, we're more in need of you than ever, Sar'nt-Major. Dammit, man, you run the ship for me – can't be without you.'

'I . . . I'm very sorry, sir.'

'Oh, I'm not casting blame!' OC Troops gave a high laugh. 'But you know that. Well – get better.' It was an order.

'Yes, sir.'

Pumphrey-Hatton made a curious trumpeting sound and turned away. From the doorway he looked back briefly. He hoped he'd put some spirit back into the RSM by his words, given him encouragement, but was in fact very certain he was looking upon imminent death. As he went along the alleyway towards the companion to the fresh air of the open decks, OC Troops encountered the ship's chief officer.

'Well met, Mr Bruton.'

'Yes, sir?'

Pumphrey-Hatton's eyes gleamed up at the chief officer. 'Two of your men. Damned ghouls. In my sar'nt-major's sick cabin – *checking him for a shroud*! I've never heard of such a thing

127

and I won't damn well have it, d'you hear me, Mr Bruton?'

'I do –'

'Any more like that, and I'll make a report to your captain. You're in charge of the seamen, are you not?'

'Yes –'

'Then damn well *take* charge of them!' Pumphrey-Hatton stalked away. Bruton collected a deckhand and sent him to find the bosun. The buck, and Bruton reckoned it was a legitimate buck this time, would be passed on.

iii

By now the cholera had made its way into the engine-room: several of Mr Stouter's engineers and greasers had gone down with it. Extra strain was being thrown onto the fit men as the watchkeeping rotas were altered and Mr Stouter himself was spending much of his time below and worrying as he did so about the possible proximity of the German surface raider. Of course, even if she was around, she might not venture within range of the heavy batteries of the *Valiant*, coming along in so stately a fashion behind the convoy. Stouter, when on deck, had looked astern at the great battleship and had been much impressed. Fighting-tops, signal bridges, admiral's and captain's bridges, a great festoon of war-camouflage steel rising to the heavens from the upper deck behind the two fo'c'sle-mounted 15-inch batteries. In Stouter's eyes she was the very embodiment of British sea power, descendant of a long line of ships that had kept Britain in full command of the world's oceans since the days of Nelson and his line-of-battle ships that had stood between Napoleon and the dominion of the world. Those few, far distant, storm-tossed British ships: a French admiral's own words, Stouter had read somewhere.

It wasn't stormy now and they were a long way from the Channel where the British fleet of old had kept its long vigil. The Arabian Sea was flat, deep blue, almost as airless as the Red Sea. An alien part of the world in which, should it come to that, to take to the boats. There were said to be cannibals

128

around in the Horn of Africa. But the escort, if the enemy came, would be sure to protect them.

Somebody else aboard the *Orlando* also had cannibals in mind: ex-Colour-Sergeant Parkinson, walking the promenade deck and meeting Petty Officer Ramm.

'Glad to leave Gardafui astern,' he said.

'How's that, then, eh?'

'You don't know about Gardafui?'

'Lighthouse there, that's all I know.'

'Ah! Unwatched – remote controlled. Didn't use to be.'

'Manned, eh? I never really thought, like.'

Parkinson nodded. 'Doesn't do, to think too much. Of course, there's a reason the light's unwatched now.'

'Go on?'

'Cannibals, in Italian Somaliland. They ate the keepers. No more were sent after that, too chancy.' Parkinson moved away, leaving Ramm to stare astern in the direction of Cape Gardafui, now out of sight and, Ramm thought, good riddance to it if that was what went on. He carried on with his work, checking round the guns, chivvying the hands, still feeling sour about the way old Perryman had turned the patch of rust against him. But checking done, he went down to see Perryman, doing his duty, half hoping things he shouldn't be hoping. When he got the news, he was quite shaken: Perryman had had a very sudden relapse, passing into the typhoid state according to the RAMC orderly.

'Very unexpected,' the orderly told Ramm. 'Very rapid. Mostly, they last longer, maybe as long as ten days.'

'Mean he's bought it, do you?' Ramm was unbelieving.

'Dead as a doornail,' the orderly said, jerking a hand towards a sheet-covered hospital bed. 'Matter of minutes before you come down.' Ramm looked from the doorway at Perryman beneath his sheet, just a lump with a protrusion where the sheet met the nose. He went away shaking his head and feeling that he was in some way to blame, thinking those thoughts about him being left in charge just when old Perryman was in the very act of kicking the bucket.

But by that afternoon, when he stood at the salute along with Commodore Kemp and watched Perryman slide from

129

under the White Ensign, he'd managed to massage his conscience quite a lot and he turned away and marched around his guns with a new authoritativeness in his step.

iv

Some died, some lived, some escaped it altogether, Ramm being one of the latter. Unexpected things happened, like Perryman's death. Rose Hardisty struggled through her state of collapse just as Jean Forrest had done. According to the medical report to the Commodore, she was likely to make it.

'Basically, a strong constitution,' Crampton said. 'And a teetotaller, which helps in cholera cases.'

'And Miss Forrest?'

'Fine, sir. More bed rest, that's all. She's been overdoing it – so had the PO Wren come to that. She too will need to be off duty for a while yet.'

Kemp nodded. 'As long as it takes, Doctor. Do you feel we're coming through it?'

'Too early to say. But the signs are reasonably good. We're probably going to get more go down with it yet, though. On the other hand, with cholera, the later cases don't seem to get it so badly. So the books say, anyhow.'

'And your personal experience?'

Crampton grinned. 'Nil. Never met it before.'

'Really? I've an idea it's just as well you didn't mention that earlier!'

Crampton was cheerful. 'That's precisely *why* I didn't mention it. The confidence of the patient is more than half the battle.'

Kemp grunted and said, 'There's a saying in the Navy. Baffle 'em with bullshit. Does that describe it?'

'Dead on, sir.'

'You're all witch-doctors,' Kemp said.

Crampton was proved right. Next day, the sick list showed 18 new cases, this time mostly amongst the ship's catering staff. Chief Steward Bliss went down with it; so did a number of galley hands, which was alarming to the lay mind but

130

Crampton tended to shrug it off. Everything was still being treated, what was left of the fresh fruit and vegetables from Aden being washed thoroughly in Condy's Fluid, and the stench of carbolic was everywhere below decks. Nevertheless, OC Troops took this news badly and sent down once more for the purser.

'Now look, Purser. The damn thing's in the galleys. And amongst the stewards. What are you going to do about it?'

'There's nothing I can do,' Rhys-Jones said, 'that isn't being done already. The doctors –'

'A *fig* for the doctors! Doctors talk as much *twaddle* as anyone else and are not necessarily to be believed. As OC Troops I'm at risk from my own steward it seems to me. And as OC Troops I can't damn well afford to be on the sick list, surely that's obvious?'

'Well, I –'

'I'll tell you what I want, Purser. I want *personal immunity*. Is that clear? Personal immunity so far as is possible. That means I want Condy's Fluid sent up here to my quarters. I'll douse my own fresh rations myself. And I'll see to it that my steward washes his hands in it the moment he enters my stateroom, each and every time. And I want special attention paid to my lavatory. Plenty of carbolic – double quantity. I trust I shall not have to repeat any of this.' Pumphrey-Hatton turned and paced his carpet, face working, eyes staring into space. Then he halted and when he spoke again his high-pitched tone was back. 'Do you know what I found this lunchtime? Do you?'

'No, I do not, Brigadier.'

'Well, then I'll tell you. It was damnable, utterly damnable.' Spittle appeared at the corner of the brigadier's mouth. 'A slug. A live – damn – slug, an *Arabian* slug. On my lettuce. How the blasted thing survived I know not, but it doesn't indicate adequate precautions having been taken. Sheer damn inefficiency and neglect of duty. And I intend having words with the Captain, I may tell you. That slug . . . it could well have had the cholera in it! Wait there.'

Pumphrey-Hatton turned away and went into his bathroom, where the makeshift shower was still in position. A moment later he returned with a plate on which sat a very limp lettuce and a slug. He thrust this at Rhys-Jones. 'There.'

131

The purser left the stateroom carrying the plate. On his way down to his office he met the Staff Captain returning from a visit to the new cases.

'What's that?' Staff Captain Main asked.

Rhys-Jones told him. 'There's a complaint going in, I'm afraid.'

'Another? But I must say, a slug's a pretty poor show.'

'Yes, it is, I agree, and I shall investigate, of course. But I would not think the slug has the cholera.'

'Nor would I, somehow. I wouldn't like to meet it on my lettuce, though.'

Rhys-Jones said, 'Yes, again I agree. But the brigadier has a bee in his bonnet, you know. I –'

'And now a slug on his lettuce.'

Rhys-Jones pursed his lips. 'I think it is no laughing matter. The brigadier, I mean. He is in a great state, a state of nerves and jumpiness. Do you know, it was almost as though he was expecting me to *order* the cholera germs not to attack him –'

'Fall 'em in and number from the right. Good God! But a lot of senior army officers are like that, Rhys-Jones. Anyway, thanks for the timely warning. I'll brief Father,' he added in reference to the Captain, 'before OC Troops surfaces. By the way what are you going to do with the slug? Keep it as evidence?'

v

Staff Captain Main was on his way to the bridge to make routine reports to the Master. But Bracewell's face stopped him in his tracks. The expression was grim and anxious.

'Staff Captain, you've appeared at the right moment. There's been a signal from the *Valiant*. She's picked up a wireless report, a mayday call from a freighter sailing independently, a Greek. A surface raider opened on her and sank her. Her position was forty-five miles sou'west.'

'And the German? Where's he heading?'

Kemp came across. He said, 'The German was on course nor' east. We might miss him, we might not –'

'I doubt if we need worry too much about the *Neuss*,' Main said. 'What with *Valiant* and our own cruiser escort?'

Kemp gave a hard laugh. 'It's not the *Neuss*, Staff Captain. It's the *Admiral Richter*. A pocket-battleship of 26,000 tons.'

TWELVE

The *Admiral Richter* was a ship name well-known to the Allied fleets. Her tours of extended duty from the Fatherland had taken her into the North and South Atlantic, and round the Cape of Good Hope into the Indian Ocean in the past; and here she was again and likely to be closing the convoy, which before long she must surely pick up on her radar. A sister ship of the *Admiral Scheer* and the *Deutschland*, she was known to mount a main armament of six 11-inch guns with a secondary armament of eight 5.9-inch, six 4.1 HA, plus eight torpedo tubes. It had been understood at the Admiralty that she was capable of a maximum speed of twenty-six knots; but even this, a comparatively high speed for a heavily armoured ship, was believed to have been exceeded. It was possible she had a reserve speed of around thirty knots. Although her guns were of lesser calibre than those of the *Valiant*, they would almost certainly prove much more effective. The German radar-controlled gunnery was admitted to be superb; and the *Valiant*'s guns were old, virtual museum pieces when set against those of the *Admiral Richter*.

'One old, slow battle-waggon,' Kemp said, 'and two cruisers. God knows, it's not much.'

'And the destroyers, sir,' Finnegan said.

'Yes. If they can get inside the guns, they could do some damage certainly, but the point is, can they? They'll meet a hail of fire all the way in. Yes, Yeoman?'

'Signal from the Flag, sir. Addressed all ships. *I intend to lie low unless brought to action. If the convoy is picked up the cruisers will stand between the merchant ships and the enemy while the destroyers carry out close torpedo attack under cover of Valiant's main armament. Message ends, sir.'*

Kemp nodded. 'Right, thank you, Yeoman. Make to all ships repeated Flag, convoy is to be ready to scatter.'

'Aye, aye, sir.'

Finnegan was hovering, a frown on his face. Kemp asked, 'Well, what is it, Finnegan?'

'The scatter order, sir. If the cruisers are to stand between us and the Heinies, do we want to be too far apart?'

'Yes, we do,' Kemp snapped.

'Sorry, sir. Just asking.'

'The cruisers are all very fine, but it's essential to disperse the targets. Then the Germans can't get us all. All right, Finnegan?'

'All right, sir.'

'Now we have other things to think about, and fast. I have the sick especially in mind. And talking of the sick, that's another reason I'm not relying on the cruisers too far. We know *Glamorgan's* got the cholera aboard. Her guns' crews will be depleted.' Kemp turned to Bracewell. 'I suggest we jump the gun, Captain, and send the ship to action stations at once. And I'd be obliged if you'd send down for all medical officers –and OC Troops.' He added, 'In the meantime, I'll speak to the men over the tannoy.'

'You think the *Richter* will pick us up, Commodore?'

'I'm damned certain she will,' Kemp said.

ii

Kemp's broadcast brought apprehension throughout the ship. This could scarcely be a worse time in which to go into action against a heavy ship. When Petty Officer Ramm heard the news it reacted deep in his guts. He'd had those thoughts about doing a *Jervis Bay* and reaping glory. Now he remembered that it had been the *Admiral Scheer* that had sunk the

135

Jervis Bay, pounding her into wreckage, bloodied with strips of human flesh and the remains of men who'd been burned in the spreading fires until their eyeballs melted. The *Scheer*'s sister ship might be all set to bring about a repeat of history, and a lot of Ramm's courage ebbed away. No peacetime liner was built to take what the *Richter* could dish out.

On the bridge, Kemp conferred with the army's medical officers and Dr Crampton. He said, 'We may have little time. I'm no medic, I need hardly say. I'm open to suggestion as to how we cope with the sick. But I'll make a suggestion of my own, and it's this: I'd like to see all of them brought up handy for the boats. It may do them no good medically, but it's a case of the lesser evil. If we have to abandon, it's going to be a question of time. You'll see the point.'

They did; any attempt to bring up the sick once the ship was under bombardment and possibly holed and on fire would be doomed. Colonel Munro of the RAMC, agreeing with the Commodore, turned to OC Troops for formal approval.

Pumphrey-Hatton said, 'Yes, yes, I agree. Much better, obviously. Where's Mr Pollock?'

Munro stared. 'Sick list, sir.'

'Oh, yes. Still?'

'Very much so. Bad prognosis I'm sorry to say.'

'Prognosis?' Pumphrey-Hatton appeared not to be entirely registering, looking away to the south-west in obvious antici-pation of the *Admiral Richter*'s arrival.

'I mean he's unlikely to recover, sir.'

'Damn! I rely on Pollock above and beyond my officers, or most of them.' Pumphrey-Hatton was starting to shake and his voice was rising. 'It's too much. Too much altogether. All the sickness and now this. Here I am. I'm dependent upon my senior RSM, the best blasted man in the brigade, and he's sick.'

'I'm afraid so, sir.' Munro's tone was formal. 'Have I your permission to carry on and bring up the sick?'

'Oh, yes, yes.'

Munro turned away, catching the eye of one of the other medical officers and giving a slight shrug as he did so. The message was clear: OC Troops could do with a sedative and a check-up but it was a case of first things first. It was going to take a lot of time to organize so many sick men up from below and range them along the embarkation deck.

Munro found an ally in Jean Forrest. She was still pale, still weak, but she had struggled out of her bunk on hearing Kemp's broadcast. She had to be useful, not just lie there being an incubus. Leaving her cabin; she all but bumped into Munro. She said she wanted to help.

'You're not fit, Miss Forrest.'

'Fit enough. I'm sure I can be of some use? They aren't going to like being moved –'

'It's for their own good.' Munro was already moving away. She caught the sleeve of his khaki-drill tunic. 'I can be with some of them, talk to them. Reassure them. I think a woman can always help.'

Munro was about to say again, and impatiently, that she wasn't fit. But then he thought: what's the point? Save her for what? They could all be dead or dying within the next hour or so. He said abruptly, 'Oh, very well then. Follow me.'

They went down to the troop decks and the various sections curtained off for use as sick bays. The troop decks themselves were emptying fast as the men were shepherded out by the platoon sergeants in orderly fashion, their life-jackets secured, tin hats on their heads, rifles held against their bodies as though they were about to go over the top in some past war, most of them with cigarettes burning. They went with chaff and laughter and here and there a snatch of ribald song, and Jean Forrest was given wolf whistles and on a couple of occasions as she brushed past the men, her bottom was pinched. She took all this as a compliment from doomed men and was glad to feel that she was still woman-looking enough to attract. She felt tears on her cheeks at the spirit of the troops as they went with military discipline to face the *Admiral Richter*'s guns.

In the sick bays there was a different feeling. The air was thick, the stench not quite overlaid by the carbolic. The very ill were put gently on stretchers and, Jean thought, were almost oblivious of what was happening. The less sick were inclined not to want to leave what seemed to them to be the security of steel bulkheads around them. In the open, there would be shell splinters flying around.

Jean put it to them: a liner's sides were paper thin. There would be no special security below. They could become trapped: they were better off handy for the boats.

'Going to come to that, is it, Miss?' a young private asked, his face pinched and yellow-looking.

She said, 'It's just a precaution. Don't forget the *Valiant's* with us.'

iii

On the bridge, all the personnel were looking out on that south-westerly bearing, watching through their binoculars for the first sign of the German's fighting-tops. Kemp was almost at the nail-biting stage: he was not going to scatter the convoy until it became unavoidable but he mustn't leave the order until it was too late. Many signals had been exchanged between the Commodore and the masters of the ammunition ships, all of them liable to go sky high if the *Admiral Richter* made contact. They had had their orders for the subsequent rendezvous after scattering if they should come through. By now the cruisers of the escort had moved across the columns to take up station on the starboard beam of the convoy, and had been joined in her slow and ponderous fashion by the old battleship whose guns were now cleared for action, the canvas hoods and the tampions removed and the great barrels swung towards where the enemy was expected to appear.

Kemp remarked, 'She's a brave sight, Finnegan.'

'Good old British Navy solidity, sir. But she does look rather like a tub, I guess.'

Kemp laughed. 'I prefer to say she has plenty of beam, and that makes for a steady gun platform. The trouble being the damn accuracy of the German gunners.'

Finnegan glanced at Kemp's face. 'Thinking of the *Hood*?'

'Yes. All over in, what, two minutes or so. Just a bloody great explosion and finish. But the *Valiant's* got more armour around her magazines. Also, her guns should outrange the *Richter's* I fancy. Heavier calibre.'

Finnegan nodded. He had the idea Kemp was talking just to

fill a gap, a gap of immense tension as the minutes ticked away. The *Hood* was history – recent, but past. There was no reason why they should go the same way. But it was good to know that the *Valiant* could outrange the Heinies. The action, if it came, would probably open with the *Valiant*'s heavy batteries.

In the engine-room, Mr Stouter was all ready for whatever might happen. All ready mentally, that was. In point of fact his engine spaces were always all ready for whatever might happen, since that was the way of engineers to whom things *did* tend to happen at awkward moments. Minor breakdowns, trouble with the ring main causing electrical faults, generators on the blink causing ditto, or the condensers reacting to being over-worked in the passengers' interest. Physically, Stouter knew there was very little he could do if a shell should smash through into the engine spaces and turn his kingdom into a fiery hell with blazing oil fuel running from shattered tanks and furnaces, and steam escaping under pressure and searing the flesh from anyone who got caught in it. About all that could be done if the worst happened was to try to get all his men up the network of ladders and into the safety – for a while anyway, with luck – of the engineers' alleyway up top, and then to the open decks handy for the boats.

Waiting for orders, waiting for the start of action, the chief engineer felt a wave of sickness.

Nerves?

He clutched at the guardrail of the starting platform, an involuntary action that was seen by his junior second engineer, acting senior second owing to the cholera.

'You all right, sir?'

'I'm okay. Everything on top line?'

'Yes, sir. I was about to report when I saw you –'

'Don't worry about me.' There was a snap in Stouter's voice, because he was now very alarmed. The sound of the engine-room seemed to have altered somehow, in an extraordinary way. It seemed to drum against his ears and to reverberate, and that increased the sick feeling. A few moments later he felt a griping pain in his stomach, enough almost to curl him in half, but with an effort he remained upright, standing with his arms rigid against the guardrail.

The sound-powered telephone from the bridge rang. It was the Captain.

'All right, Chief?'

'All right, sir.'

'*Valiant* reports contact and is altering course. Stand by for fireworks, Chief.' Bracewell cut the connection. Stouter wiped sweat from his face and neck with a handful of cotton-waste. So now this was it: action imminent. A bloody good time for the cholera to strike! Well, the cholera would have to wait, that was all about it. He was needed where he was. In any case he might be dead from other causes, any moment now.

iv

PO Wren Hardisty was shifted from her cabin with the others and set into a deck chair on the embarkation deck. She was feeling better, a little but not much, but at least she felt she had a grip on life again if only the Germans would leave her alone. First Officer Forrest, on her way below to help bring more men up on deck, stopped by her chair.

'You're looking better, PO.'

'Yes, ma'am, thank you. Don't you go overdoing it, now.'

Jean smiled down at her. 'No, nanny.'

'Oh, dear, ma'am! Did I sound like that?'

'Yes, you did, and why not? Nannies are comfortable persons, good to have around. Now I'll say the same thing: don't *you* overdo it, Rose. No thoughts about getting up to help, and that's an order.'

She went away, back to her self-imposed task. Miss Hardisty was too overcome to say any more before she went. Miss Forrest had called her Rose. She didn't ever remember that happening before. It was just like the old days, when she had in fact been a nanny, and the master and mistress had called her Rose while the children called her nanny and the below-stairs servants called her Miss Hardisty. Having those days brought back she cried a little, partly from sheer weakness, partly from nostalgia. She thought of little Master Donald in his tank in the Western Desert, giving orders and that, and fighting that Rommel. She hoped he was all right and looking after himself, taking care to air his vests. He'd always been such a little rascal. Rapscallion, she'd called him when he was naughty. She blushed, even now, when she thought about the fuckum bloosance.

Out of earshot but not out of sight, two of Miss Hardisty's current charges giggled together: in this predicament you had to have a laugh or you'd go round the bend.

'Crying – did you see?'

'Who?'

'The old cow.'

'Didn't think she could.' To some, all PO Wrens were akin to gunner's mates – quarried, not born of woman. 'What's up with her?'

'Scared, probably. So am I come to that.' The girl paused, then said somewhat diffidently, 'Let's go and talk to her. She's not a bad old stick.'

The other girl murmured something about her friend wanting mummy's comfort, but they went over and stopped as Jean Forrest had done, and talked to Miss Hardisty who realized their own need. They squatted on the deck by her side and she told them not to worry, the Navy would protect them, and back in London the King and Queen were depending on them all to keep smiling through, the King and Queen who'd had a bomb on Buckingham Palace and hadn't turned a hair, just stiffened their backs and their upper lips and carried on, going round the dirt and rubble of the East End bringing cheer and courage to the bombed-out victims of the war . . . they were embarrassed and tended to giggle again. It was so typical of the old girl, but what she said did help and it was perfectly true that the King and Queen had refused to leave London in the blitz when they could have had every excuse to do so.

Miss Hardisty was saying what a wonderful man Winston Churchill was, him and his cigar and his V for Victory sign and his derisive remarks about Hitler and Mussolini, when a matter of two miles on the convoy's starboard beam the heavy guns of the *Valiant* went into action.

The first sighting report from the *Glamorgan* extended towards the enemy had come in just a matter of minutes before and the bridge personnel had been too busy to make a broadcast. From the Commodore the order had gone out to the convoy to scatter as soon as the *Valiant* had reported contact; the armaments carriers had swung away to port before steadying to get clear north-west of the German guns. *Orlando* continued on her course until the other ships were on safe bearings, then Bracewell too altered to port. The zig-zag was maintained in hopes of throwing off the *Admiral Richter*'s gunners. As the *Valiant* opened in a sudden belch of flame and smoke the destroyers were seen to be increasing speed to their maximum and going bravely in towards the enemy, while the two cruisers stood guard over the scattering ships of the convoy. From the *Orlando*'s bridge the *Admiral Richter* was as yet invisible over the horizon, though within the next two minutes a report from the masthead lookout came down.

'Enemy in sight, sir!'

Almost on the heels of this report there was a whistle overhead, a whistle like an express train coming closer and then passing on. All the men on the bridge ducked instinctively. Then a great waterspout rose in the ocean, around four cables on the *Orlando*'s beam.

'Ranging shot,' Kemp said. 'And a good one at that.'

THIRTEEN

By this time all watertight doors had been shut and all boats lowered to the guardrails of the embarkation deck with the ship's officers and petty officers standing by the falls with the lowerers. Below, the fire parties were ready with the hoses. Petty Officer Ramm was making the rounds of the guns, moving fast, exhorting the guns' crews with words of wisdom about making every shell count.

'Every bloody shell,' Ramm said. 'God knows we haven't got Woolwich bloody Arsenal aboard.'

'Whites of their eyes, PO?' a leading seaman asked, winking at one of the gunnery rates.

'Don't be bloody cheeky. There's no time for it. Pull that anti-flash gear down over your mug, set an example as a leading 'and, can't you?'

Ramm went on his way; behind him the leading hand muttered 'Daft sod,' and adjusted his anti-flash gear. Petty officers were a pain, if it had been Perryman he'd have been looking for rust which he wouldn't have found. As Ramm went for'ard, another shell screamed overhead. This time those on the bridge felt the wind of its passage.

'Closer,' Bracewell said as they watched the fall and the waterspout. 'Too ruddy close!'

They did what they could, which could only be to keep up the zig-zag; that, and get the utmost speed out of the engines. Bracewell had already passed the order for that. He wouldn't press the chief engineer further: he would be doing his best.

143

Meanwhile, down below, Stouter's acting senior second had suggested that the ship's surgeon take a look at him.

'He's too busy . . . and so am I, God damn it!' The sickness racked him, the pain in his gut was intense. Something had to give and it did. This devastated him: he was unclean, a horrible sight. Soon after this he was reduced to clinging onto the guardrail, hanging over it rather than just clinging, and he felt his senses slipping away. The acting senior second took over then, detailed three men to steady the chief up the ladders, and rang the bridge.

'Middleton here, sir. I'm taking over below. The chief's down with the cholera . . . or I reckon it's that, anyway.'

Bracewell put down the phone and looked grim. He passed the news to the Commodore. He said, 'We'll cope – or they will below. Middleton's a good man, according to the chief. But it's bloody bad luck.'

On the embarkation deck OC Troops was facing more bad luck. Moving along beside the waiting boats, followed by his brigade major, he came upon what looked like a corpse, just as stiff as one, but which he recognized after another shocked look as RSM Pollock. There seemed to be nothing left of him, skin and bone, the skin hanging in folds as he lay in a Neil Robertson stretcher, handy for one of the lifeboats, tended by a medical orderly.

'How is he?' OC Troops asked the man, who had come to attention.

'Conscious, sir.'

'Yes, but –' Pumphrey-Hatton broke off, taking in the burden of the orderly's words: he didn't want to say in the hearing of a conscious man that he'd just about had it. Pumphrey-Hatton spoke instead to Pollock.

'You'll be all right, Pollock. Fresh air, you know.'

'Sir.' The word was little more than a croak, but the RSM, Pumphrey-Hatton saw, was doing his best to lie to attention as the patients in the military hospitals were accustomed to do when the medical officer made his rounds.

Pumphrey-Hatton gave a cough. 'Yes, well. We'll see that you're first into the boats if we abandon.'

'Sir. Thank you . . . but there's the women, sir. The Wrens . . . they must be first, sir.'

'Ah yes, yes. That's the tradition, of course. Well – get better. As I said before, I need you.' OC Troops passed on, marvelling that Pollock had lasted this far when he was clearly in such a low state. As he moved away, he was overtaken by the brigade major, who saluted and barred his passage. 'Yes? What is it, Major?'

'The sar'nt-major, sir. He has something more to say.'

'To me?'

'Yes, sir.'

Pumphrey-Hatton turned back with a touch of impatience. The sick shouldn't overtire themselves, for one thing. 'Well, Pollock, you wished to speak to me.'

'With your permission, sir.' The voice was croakier than ever and very faint now. Pumphrey-Hatton had to bend close to hear it. 'Carlisle, sir. The regiment . . . the castle. My wife sir. And the children.'

Pumphrey-Hatton frowned. The RSM was wandering, he was disjointed. 'Yes, yes. Your family. Of course –'

'To be looked after, sir. My regiment . . . Border. If they're told, sir. If they're told . . .'

'Oh, of course they'll be told, Mr Pollock. Don't *bestir* yourself. The families are always looked after, you know that, surely.'

He turned away again; he had much to do to ensure that the embarkation in the boats went without fuss or difficulty. Many of the men would have to make use of the Carley floats that were ready in the slides to be shot into the water if and when the abandon order came. He spoke to the brigade major about Pollock. 'Make a note, Major. Pollock's family – his regiment to be told – the depot to be told. Of his death.'

'He's not dead yet, sir.'

'Oh, don't argue, Major, I've so much to think about.' OC Troops jumped as an immense explosion came from somewhere on the port beam. 'Good God! What was that?'

'Ammunition ship blown up,' the brigade major said, staring in horror. Caught before she had moved out of the *Admiral Richter*'s fifteen-mile range on the scatter order, the ship had disintegrated. The ship herself couldn't be seen. There was a heavy pall of thick black smoke shot through with

145

roaring flames of red and orange, a fearsome sight. The brigade major remarked that the bottom must have been blown out of her. She was going down like a lump of fragmented concrete.

Pumphrey-Hatton turned away with a bad attack of the shakes. His face said that he knew only too well that the *Orlando* could well be next. He was not the only one; not for the first time since the convoy had left the Clyde, the terrible ambience of death on so total a scale beneath the smoke and flame had brought for a while the silence of awe to the crowded decks. Then they all seemed to start talking at once; Pumphrey-Hatton believed he detected a difference this time. The sudden voices gave him the thought that panic could come and the men could rush the boats. They'd been through air and submarine attack in the Mediterranean as well as in the North Atlantic soon after leaving the Clyde, but to come under the huge guns of a battleship was a very different experience. The shells seemed to come from nowhere, right out of the blue. And some were coming closer.

Pumphrey-Hatton saw the falls of shot on his way to the bridge. He spoke to Kemp. 'The German's concentrating on us now, I fancy.'

'With one of her turrets only, I believe. She's also engaging the *Valiant*, Brigadier. As for us – we're a troop transport. I expected we'd take the brunt.'

Pumphrey-Hatton nodded several times then spoke about his anxiety: possible panic along the troop-laden decks. 'They're jumpy,' he said.

'Naturally. Jumpiness isn't panic. And I'm sure you have good NCOs.'

'Oh yes. Indeed. A damn pity about Pollock, though.'

'I wouldn't worry about panic,' Kemp said. He brought up his binoculars; he didn't want to go on discussing panic and wondered why OC Troops should broach the subject at all, especially with the Commodore. Any incipient panic would be nipped in the bud by the ship's officers and senior ratings, as well as by the NCOs and redcaps. He watched the brigadier go with his jerky walk to the other wing of the bridge where he approached Bracewell. Kemp fancied Pumphrey-Hatton might be trying to fight down personal feelings of panic, airing the subject in the hopes of steadying himself. The matter went right out of his mind in the next instant when he saw a vivid flash come from the quarterdeck of the *Valiant*, now some five miles to the south.

Lambert reported. '*Valiant* hit aft, sir!'

Kemp stared through his binoculars. There was a lot of smoke and some flame and so far as he was able to make out the after turret had taken a direct hit from the *Admiral Richter*, in which case two of the old battleship's 15-inch guns were now out of action, a quarter of her main armament gone. If the fire bit down into the shell handling rooms and the after magazines . . . that didn't bear thinking about. Meanwhile the *Valiant* was still under way and appeared to have her steering under control as well. That indicated no residual damage to her engines, or to her screws or rudder. And she was maintaining her fire from all remaining LA guns, the 6-inch barbettes along her starboard side appearing to be joining in now, judging from the puffs of smoke rising above her main deck.

Kemp was thinking to himself that for the moment at any rate the *Admiral Richter* was being fully engaged by the *Valiant* and that the *Orlando* was in for a respite, when another shell screamed across, lower than the previous ones, its path taking it slap into the mainmast which crashed down to the boat deck and then lay half over the side, its top hamper slamming into the swung-out boats along the embarkation deck. There had been some casualties: yells and cries came up to the bridge and Kemp saw OC Troops rush to the starboard ladder and start shouting down to the troops.

Then another shell sliced across the troopship's stern, there was an eruption of smoke and flame and a shatteringly close explosion that rocked the bridge and sent shock waves right through the ship. A surge of troops came for'ard at the rush, as Kemp saw when he leaned dangerously out from the bridge wing. A report came up that there was fighting along the embarkation deck.

Panic?

Pumphrey-Hatton was still shouting uselessly from the

147

head of the bridge ladder. No-one was taking any notice of him.

ii

When the shell hit aft, Petty Officer Ramm went at the double from his action station at the for'ard 6-inch, pounding up the ladders and along the boat deck, avoiding the embarkation deck and its surging, fighting troops. Reaching what had been the after gun he found just one survivor of its crew and him only just about alive. Ramm squatted on the deck and took the man's head in his hands. There were mangled bodies that told their own story. There was an arm that had been blown from the trunk, wearing the tattered remnant of a short-sleeved white shirt, Number Thirteen rig. The remnant carried a blue badge of rank: the leading seaman in charge of the gun. Of the rest of him there was no sign. Blood was everywhere, dripping from shattered steel. There was a gaping hole in the deck where the gun-mounting had been. The deck itself was ripped up, the woodwork burning. The after ends of the upper decks were black and twisted, and along them there were more casualties, men who had caught the blast. The medical teams were coming aft now, with Neil Robertson stretchers.

Ramm straightened and, almost unseeing, moved away from the hole where the 6-inch had been. His feet slithered on a big patch of blood, and, reaching out an arm towards a twisted stanchion for support, he contacted something sticky, something hairy. He looked. It was a head, just a detached head that had somehow been blown into the twist of the stanchion and had become lodged. Ramm just about reached the ship's side before he brought his stomach up. Then, pale and shaking, he made his way back for'ard again. That was where he could still be of use: all the close-range weapons had gone from the after end of the boat deck.

148

PO Wren Hardisty had been submerged in the rush from aft along the embarkation deck, where now four of the lifeboats hung in shreds of woodwork, rendered useless by the fall of the mainmast and the banging of the cross-trees that had broken away to dangle over the edge of the boat deck above. Miss Hardisty's deck chair collapsed beneath her and as she lay helpless a number of feet trod on her, no notice being taken of her cries.

Not until a tall, straight-backed figure emerged from a door in the bulkhead close by and gave a roar of rage and shoved through to her assistance. Nightwatchman Parkinson couldn't believe his eyes at seeing the mêlée. He grabbed a passing sergeant by the arm and swung him round.

'What's all this, then?'

'Look for yourself, mate –'

'I'm looking. I'm seeing a piss-poor twerp wearing sergeant's chevrons and failing to take charge as he ought.'

'Who're you, then, bloody nightwatchman to talk –'

'Ex-Colour Sar'nt Parkinson, Royal Marines. Eastney Barracks. Right. Now then.' Parkinson took a deep breath, still hanging onto the sergeant. 'Get your mates together and stop this bloody stampede. If you don't, I'll have you on the bridge with a report to the Master and OC Troops and have you broken to the ranks.'

He gave the sergeant a heavy shove, sending him smack into another man trying to struggle past. Parkinson raised his voice in a mighty shout and barred the way with his big body. He got hold of two privates, holding one in each hand.

'There's a woman here.' He was almost standing on Miss Hardisty by this time. 'Get her inside the bulkhead, through the door. Lift her careful, she may be injured. *Get moving!*'

Miss Hardisty was carried through. Parkinson followed behind, closing the door on the mob. He wiped sweat from his face. He said, 'What a perishing carry-on, I never see the like! You hurt, PO?'

'No, I – I don't think so. Only bruised. Oh, dear! Thank you so much . . .'

'Don't mention it. I'll stay by till you're on your feet.'

'Oh no, please don't bother, I'm sure you've other things to do.' She was very breathless; she'd been very frightened by the troops' behaviour, such as she would never have associated with trained soldiers. She said, 'Of course, it's the cholera.'

'Eh? What is?'

'The way they behaved. There's been so much anxiety about the cholera, and –'

'No excuse,' Parkinson said.

'Well, I don't know . . . what's going to happen now, do you think? To the ship?'

Parkinson was encouraging. 'She'll be all right. I put my trust in the skipper.'

'Yes. That's what I tell my girls. But there are things even captains can't guard against.'

'There's always God.'

'Oh, I know, and I do really and truly believe. I've been praying ever since the first broadcast. I'm sure I'm not the only one. The trouble is, God must also be worrying about the Germans, and –'

'If He is, then He's wasting precious time. Them Jerries aren't 'uman. You all right now, PO?'

'Yes, thank you very much, Mr Parkinson. But I think I'll stay where I am rather than go back out there.'

iv

Nightwatchman Parkinson had gone back through the door to assist the army's NCOs, who seemed much in need of it. But order was restored fairly quickly when the staff sergeants and company sergeant-majors got in amongst the troops and were not too particular as to how they dealt with what had had the appearance of a situation leading to mutiny. The officers were keeping out of it until the NCOs had restored control. There were times when officers were superfluous and even inflammatory, and if there was rough stuff being doled out by the NCOs then the turning of the blind eye was the sensible thing to do.

150

Pumphrey-Hatton had remained in his stance at the head of the bridge ladder throughout. He had contributed nothing to the restoration of discipline, but when it was all over he appeared to think that the mere fact of his visible eye taking it all in had won the day. He talked again about panic and the need for firmness to bring it under control. He was almost cocky, believing the feared panic to have materialized and been dealt with so fast it wouldn't recur.

Reports were coming in from the various after sections of the ship. There had been no damage below, other than the fact of the hole where the 6-inch mounting had been. There had been casualties at the after ends of the boat deck, embarkation deck and promenade decks but the army medical details were coping. The ship was seaworthy and was still moving at her maximum speed when Kemp saw another hit on the *Valiant*, this time immediately before the midship superstructure. It was evidently a heavy calibre shell from the German's main armament and the results as seen from a distance looked devastating. The blast went upwards and fire spread fast towards the battleship's compass platform. On the heels of the hit there was another one right aft, another heavy shell that took the quarter fair and square. Smoke billowed, shot through with flames.

Kemp said, 'She's swinging off course!'

Bracewell was beside him. 'Steering gone by the look of it.'

'Probably got the rudder. Twisted the shafts too. If that's happened, she won't even be able to steer by main engines. She'll lie at the *Richter*'s mercy . . . be pounded to pieces.'

There was nothing they could do but watch and hope as the old battleship started to go round in circles and then gradually slowed and lost her way through the water. Kemp believed that his diagnosis had been right: shafts twisted, rudder gone. One of the cruisers of the escort was altering now, racing towards the stricken ship. The destroyers were still making at speed towards the *Admiral Richter* on their errand to get off their torpedoes, but Kemp knew that they would be moving into a curtain of gunfire. They were the last hope; with the *Valiant* crippled though firing still, the German was going to have it virtually all his own way unless the destroyers could get their tin fish into the massive hull.

151

Bracewell, watching the pathetic contortions of the *Valiant*, said suddenly, 'More trouble, Commodore.'

'What is it this time?'

Bracewell pointed towards the south-east. 'Just look at that.'

Kemp did. He saw a long, low line of cloud, very black, very threatening, building up along the horizon and starting to extend. Curious colourings fingered along the sky above the cloud, red and purple, green and orange. Kemp said, 'Talk about filthy luck! First the cholera, then the *Richter*. Now a typhoon by the look of it. We must have a jonah aboard.' He paused. 'I've never known a typhoon as far north as this, Bracewell. Have you?'

'No.' Typhoons, hurricanes as they were called in the West Indies and the Caribbean, were to be expected in the Indian Ocean and also in the Bay of Bengal, though properly they belonged to the China seas and the Philippines. But to find them here was something rare.

'Someone, somewhere,' Kemp said heavily, 'doesn't like us very much. You'd think the bloody Met men would have issued a warning!'

'We couldn't have done much about it, Commodore. And it'll hit the *Richter* as well as us.'

'It won't help the convoy. We'll be all over the show by the time that lot's passed through.'

Bracewell was about to speak when Sub-Lieutenant Finnegan gave a shout down from monkey's island above the wheelhouse where he'd been checking the crews of the close-range weapons mounted for the protection of the bridge. 'I guess the destroyers have got through, sir! The *Richter*'s concentrating her secondary armament on –' He broke off.

'What is it, Finnegan?' Kemp called.

Finnegan was beside himself with excitement now. 'The *Richter*, sir! A bloody big explosion on the waterline, port side for'ard. They've got the bastard!'

The word spread; there was a storm of cheering along the decks. PO Wren Hardisty emerged from cover, chancing the embarkation deck again.

'Whatever's happened?' she asked breathlessly.

Someone told her. She said, 'I knew we'd be all right. I always knew it.'

'It's not over yet, missus.'

'PO,' Miss Hardisty said automatically. 'Not missus.' The man, a soldier, didn't pay any attention. A moment later the tannoy came alive and Miss Hardisty heard Commodore Kemp's voice, which cheered her even more.

Kemp said, 'This is the Commodore speaking. As I gather you already know, the *Admiral Richter* has been hit. She's been hit for'ard by torpedoes from one of our destroyers. She is down by the head and losing way but is still firing with her main and secondary armaments. In the meantime you'll have seen that the *Valiant* is badly crippled and unable to steer. It's a case of honours even, but I expect more torpedo hits from the destroyers. I have one more item of news. We are being borne down upon by a typhoon from the south-east. This will affect the course of the action. When the storm hits us, I shall want all men off the open decks – you'll not go below to the troop decks but will muster under your officers and NCOs in the main lounges. You'll be tightly packed but that can't be helped. Also, the boats will be hoisted to the davit heads and secured against the weather with griping bands passed. Don't worry about this. It's a necessary precaution and in any case we couldn't get any lifeboats away under typhoon conditions. That is all.'

The tannoy clicked off.

Miss Hardisty, not waiting for the wind to arrive, mustered her girls – they were all more or less together in a bunch in accordance with her own orders – and shoo-ed them inside the superstructure. They found a corner of the main A deck lounge and re-arranged some chairs and sofas and sat down to form a close-knit group, but Miss Hardisty knew they would have to pack in much tighter when the troops poured in.

'The order was *mine* to give, Commodore.'

'I'm sorry. You weren't on the bridge.'

'I was below, but not for long. Dammit, you should have waited!'

'Do you disagree with my order, Brigadier?'

Pumphrey-Hatton's face twitched. 'No, no! I consider it sensible enough –'

'Then what's all the fuss about?'

'Fuss?'

'Yes, fuss. We're in action, Brigadier, and are about to meet bad weather – very bad weather. There's no time for ceremonial in a typhoon, as you're about to find out for yourself. You'll find life uncomfortable until it's moved past.'

Pumphrey-Hatton gave a gasp, looked furious, found the right words wouldn't come, and turned sharply on his heel. He went across to the port bridge wing, his spindly body jerking with suppressed fury. Kemp sighed inwardly; once again, he'd got on the wrong side of OC Troops. He should have bitten down hard on his tongue, but the fellow's manner irritated him beyond endurance and he felt he had enough to worry about without adding Pumphrey-Hatton's maddening military tantrums to his mind. In any case the safety of personnel at sea was his and Bracewell's responsibility, not that of OC Troops, at any rate not primarily. Sea officers knew what they were about. And some decisions had to be made fast. Like now: Kemp's weather eye had told him the typhoon would hit in rather less than half-an-hour. When it did, the *Orlando* would be tossed about like a cork.

In the event the typhoon was beaten to it by the *Admiral Richter*. This time there was no preliminary scream, no rush of wind. The 11-inch shell took the *Orlando* smack amidships, low down at the end of its trajectory, plunging directly against the ship's plates alongside the engine-room.

FOURTEEN

No-one who was actually in the engine-room escaped, though there were survivors, miraculously, from the boiler-rooms. The miracle was not a kindly one, however: few of those erstwhile survivors were going to live. The burns from the blazing fuel oil were horrendous. The black gang had been brought out at great risk to the bosun and his deck hands, brought out through a shattered bulkhead through which the fire hoses were sending their jets of water to damp down the raging fires inside. Dr Crampton went below himself and tended the burns cases with assistance from the RAMC. In the engine-room itself there was total destruction; the place was no more than a mass of twisted steel, the ladders to the air lock all gone, the shafts broken, the dials and gauges a shapeless mass had there been anyone alive to see. Except for the radio room, which had its own source of electricity supplying its own generator, all electric power throughout the ship had gone.

Chief Engineer Stouter, removed earlier to his cabin, was too sick to realize the full extent of it. With the fires beneath his cabin so far increasing their hold on the ship he was moved again, this time into a camp bed in the military officers' cabin alleyway on B deck.

Bracewell, his face grey with anxiety, took the reports on the bridge. Staff Captain Main had been down himself, had left the chief officer in charge. Main was blackened, his hair singed, arms and hands showing burns and blisters.

'It's a shambles, sir. Touch and go if we get the fires under control . . . they're doing wonders down there.'

'Are we making water, Staff Captain?'

Main said, 'A little. The carpenter's sounding round. The after collision bulkhead's holding, but only just. There are some sprung rivets and some seepage, but that'll help the fire parties.'

'If the bulkhead goes –'

'We'll have had it.'

A simple statement of fact, no less. They would go down for sure. Bracewell conferred with the Commodore. He said, 'By rights I should abandon. Or stand by to any moment.'

'But not with the weather coming in.'

'Hardly.'

That was the problem: the fires might be brought under control; that was at the moment unpredictable. What was wholly predictable was that any attempt to abandon would lead to disaster, a suicide move in fact. And inside the next five minutes the storm was going to hit them and then there could be no possible hope of getting boats away, as Kemp had broadcast on the tannoy not long before.

'We just have to sit it out,' Bracewell said. Already the hurricane had overtaken the engaged battleships, the cruisers and the destroyers. They were invisible from the *Orlando*'s bridge, as were the other merchant ships, the armaments carriers for the eventual supply of the Fourteenth Army fighting in Burma. Everything was now in a state of chaos, of total flux. As the Staff Captain went below again towards the fires, the day darkened and the storm, moving swiftly across the final gap, struck the *Orlando* like another battering from the *Admiral Richter*. Currently, as it happened, the ship was heading into the wind and sea. For a while she remained there; but not for long. The typhoon's fury came suddenly a little on the port bow. Only a little; but the fury and force of the wind and sea were such that the ship was taken as though in a giant's fist and laid over, wrenched to starboard, the bow lifting to the thrust of the waves, and twisting, before plunging right under so far and so deep that the sea rose up along the fo'c'sle and smashed at the base of the midship

156

superstructure, rising for a while as far as just below the Master's deck before it fell away, much of it making its way aft, washing along the embarkation deck and then finding the hole left by the smashed gun-mounting and pouring down into the ship's innards.

ii

The lounges, now unlit, were murderous. The sudden lift and surge had sent men off their feet, flinging them in all directions on top of one another. Furniture, secured to the deck in many cases, broke free and hurtled around, unstoppable. A grand piano took off, the piano round which the brigade's officers had sung popular tunes to keep their spirits up through the cholera; it shifted bodily as the deck canted so sharply and came down on a group of men struggling on the deck, breaking bones and heads, a bloody scene to add to the other horrors. Miss Hardisty clung to a stanchion, a big pillar that ran from deck to deckhead, clung for her life in the near dark. Some of her girls were hanging onto the same pillar, others were holding onto the PO Wren herself. Some of the girls had disappeared in the mêlée. Those with Miss Hardisty were crying; she was crying herself and trying not to let it show. Petty officers didn't cry, she told herself fiercely, they had to set an example.

But now she was desperately afraid. She didn't believe the ship could possibly come through. First the German shell, then this. The ship must be filling up with water and, sogged from top to bottom, would sink. There was the very atmosphere of death. For one thing the stifling heat had gone and had been replaced with a terrible cold that was worse than the heat, the worse for being, to her at any rate, totally unexpected and so sudden. It didn't seem right, it didn't seem human. There was evil in it, Miss Hardisty thought.

Then salvation of a kind came. The ship steadied. And someone spoke to her, a voice coming over the shriek of the gale that was now inside the lounge, having shattered the big windows on its way in.

'All right, PO. It's all right. For a while anyway. Ship's sort of held in irons if you get my meaning.'

'Oh, dear!' Miss Hardisty felt ex-Colour Sergeant Parkinson's arms going round her and unfastening her hands from the pillar. 'Are you sure?'

'Yes, PO. You can let go now. All of you.'

Miss Hardisty let go. She teetered a little on her legs, which felt very shaky, and Parkinson steadied her. She asked how the fighting was going, but Parkinson didn't know. Nobody knew, he said, all the ships were in the same boat, so to speak. None of them could see each other and the battle would have been suspended.

'*Force majeure*,' he said. 'That's the way of typhoons. Beat navies, they do. You just have to ride 'em out, the buggers . . . begging your pardon, PO.'

Miss Hardisty was so upset she hadn't even registered the word. She asked, 'How long will it last?'

'Depends on its speed and depth. Maybe not long. I've been in 'em before, Indian Ocean, China-side. Want something to do, do you, PO, you and your young ladies?'

She said, yes they did. They had to keep their minds off their predicament.

'Good. I knew I could rely on you. There's been a grand piano loose. It's brought a lot of injuries and the medics have their hands full with burns from the engine-room. That, and the cholera cases. Come with me, eh?'

Miss Hardisty collected her girls, made a quick count and found six missing, but this wasn't the time to go and look for them. Parkinson was pushing through the troops and Miss Hardisty had to keep close. They reached the piano, lying smashed on its side. It had been lifted away from the men beneath. There were men with broken arms and legs, crushed hands, crushed ribs and stomachs, and two seemed already dead with their heads covered with table-cloths that showed a good deal of blood seeping through. Miss Hardisty was in a mental whirl but her innate compassion took charge, and she sat on the deck and talked to the men like a caring mother. She and the Wren ratings, casting aside modesty, removed some of their clothing and tore it into strips to use as makeshift bandages to hold broken bones in place for the doctors when they could get around to it. With no medical knowledge really, just her experience as a nanny of tending children who had fallen over and damaged themselves, Miss Hardisty could only hope she wasn't making matters worse.

While she was doing her first-aid act the tannoy came on. The system was fed through the radio room's generator. The calm voice of Commodore Kemp came over loud and clear.

'I want to give you all the facts,' Kemp was saying. 'The fires below are being brought under control. You needn't worry on that score. But the engine-room is out of action and will remain so. Also, we're making a certain amount of water. I believe the pumps will cope, though without power they're having to be worked by hand, by relays of men. OC Troops has authorized the use of the military to back up the ship's company, and orders for rotas will be issued shortly, I understand, from the orderly room. However, I have to warn you that it may become necessary to abandon once the typhoon's past. As to the action, we have no idea how it's going – or rather, how it was left, since it certainly won't be going on now. With luck, the *Admiral Richter* will be far, far away when the weather moderates.' Kemp paused. 'There's one more thing I have to tell you and I'm very sorry it's necessary. Very sorry indeed. RSM Pollock has died. That is all . . . I shall speak to you again as things develop.'

iii

A buzz of comment had run through the lounges and other jam-packed spaces. Bull's Bollocks had been a martinet with a mind that had appeared rigid as rock to those of the troops who had joined as conscripts and others with no experience of pre-war military machines. But he had always been fair, always straightforward: you knew precisely where you stood with him. So, mostly, he was going to be missed, especially in the orderly room which was now a shambles of upturned desks and scattered documents and where the rota for the pumps would have to be worked out. There was comment

159

also about the other contents of the Commodore's broadcast: mostly around what he hadn't said. What was going to happen to a troopship without her main engines, whether or not the pumps kept her afloat?

This question was asked, somewhat rhetorically, by one of the army doctors of Jean Forrest, who was still helping out. He seemed to think that on account of the two-and-a-half blue stripes of rank on her uniform she would know the answers of the sea.

She said helplessly, 'I really don't know.'

'We can't just float around the Arabian Sea, getting nowhere.'

'No . . .'

'Damn great target, if there are any submarines around. And the *Richter* could still be close when we come through. If we come through.'

'Oh,' she said, 'we'll come through, don't worry.'

The doctor grinned. 'You sound confident, Miss Forrest. I like confidence. It's my stock-in-trade too. Or should be. Why are *you* so confident?'

She said simply, 'Because of Commodore Kemp.'

'You really mean that, don't you?'

'Yes,' she said. 'Yes, I do. I think he's wonderful. Really great.'

He gave her a sweeping look: she was very attractive. And there had been something in her tone that he recognized. Not infrequently he'd heard that tone himself, from nurses who'd thought he, too, was great. He grinned again and said, 'Lucky man,' and noted afterwards that she had blushed scarlet and had changed the subject quickly. He hoped she was right about her Commodore Kemp. Himself, he couldn't feel quite the same certainty – but then he wasn't a woman. Maybe this time a woman's intuition, or whatever, would be proved right. It was always a hope.

In the orderly room a note was made on the word of the brigade major that RSM Pollock's regimental depot at Carlisle was to be informed: The Border Regiment was not part of the embarked brigade – Pollock had been on secondment for troopship staff duties. The brigade major hoped his regiment would look after the widow and children. When they came through, if they did, then he would write personally to Mrs Pollock. One of the things he would not put in that letter was that the regimental sergeant-major had not been accorded military honours at the last. That had not been possible, nor had a proper committal: Pollock, who was going to die anyway, had not in fact died from the cholera. He had been caught, helpless in his Neil Robertson stretcher, by the surge of sea when the first of the typhoon had struck. He had simply been washed overboard, his body bouncing down the companion at the after end of the embarkation deck and thence over the side. A number of men, themselves fighting for their lives against the enormous weight of water, had seen a body go by but had not until later realized that it had been the RSM.

An undignified way for any RSM to leave this life. But the brigade major thought wryly that Mr Pollock would make up for it when reporting to the gates of heaven. '*RSM Pollock. Sir! Late The Border Regiment, on detachment from Earth, reporting for duty.*' There might even be the odd scruffy saint, ordered in no uncertain terms to stand still . . .

'Pumping rotas,' the brigade major said briskly. 'It's up to us to help save the ship.' He spoke with a confidence that he was far from feeling. Even he, a landsman, guessed that the ship was making too much water for her safety. There was a different feel, not just the feel of a ship rolling and lurching without power but a nerve-racking deadness, an inertness that gave a strong feeling of unease.

This had been more professionally remarked on the bridge. The carpenter's report to the chief officer had been that the ship was making water amidships to the extent that soon she would be riding dangerously low. The situation might alter for the better once the army had pulled itself together and organized the troops to the pumps. Meanwhile the working alleyways below the accommodation decks were beginning to flood, and the lower accommodation decks were themselves at risk. They were now out of bounds to the troops, with the ship's petty officers, assisted by the army NCOs, standing guard to ensure the order was obeyed, stopping men not on duty at the pumps from going below to salvage personal effects, photographs and so on.

For some while now, again a miracle Kemp thought, the ship had remained more or less steady – held, as Parkinson had assured Miss Hardisty, in irons, rather like the old-time square-riggers that had been held by the wind and sea to a course from which the strength of the elements would not permit them to alter.

But a change was coming. They could all see that when the bows began to swing, to veer off to starboard. Bracewell went to the tannoy and issued a warning.

'The ship is about to lie across the wind and sea. Without power on the main engines there is nothing we can do to prevent it. Everyone throughout the ship must hang on to whatever they can find.' When the cloud had first appeared over the horizon lifelines had been hastily rigged along the open decks, where now only the ship's crew would be allowed until the storm was past.

'Touch and go now,' Bracewell said after his broadcast. 'Touch and go till the weather moderates . . . all the way through.'

Kemp nodded. At his side Finnegan asked, 'What's next, sir?'

'Next? Don't ask me, sub! We're in the hands of God from now on. You've never seen a typhoon, have you?'

'Hurricanes in the Caribbean, sir – same thing.'

'From seaward?'

'Ashore, sir.'

'There's a difference,' Kemp said briefly. 'The question is whether we survive the broach-to, or not. All right, Finnegan?'

'I guess so, sir.'

'Hang on, then.'

Kemp held fast himself to a stanchion, wedged in one corner of the wheelhouse. Bracewell was in the other. The senior second officer who had the watch was by the binnacle, holding on with the helmsman. Although they were in shelter, they had to shout to make themselves heard. The shriek of the wind was horrifying, carrying its own hint of terror. The seas were dropping aboard, coming more and more to port as the ship's head began to go to starboard, thundering down on the bower anchors and the slips and bottle-screws, surging to starboard and aft over the break of the fo'c'sle to drop down on the windlass beneath, or over that to crash down on the fore cargo hatches, surging round the feet of the derricks, swilling up, building up against the base of the midship superstructure. The ship was lurching, wallowing, thrown over now to starboard bodily as the scend of the sea and the tearing wind, blowing now at something around 130 knots, pushed her over and over. Kemp and Bracewell watched the gauge that showed the degree of list; Bracewell's knuckles stood out white as the indicator hovered close to the point of no return, the angle of list from which there would be no recovery. There was a tense moment when the indicator touched that danger mark, and stayed there for what seemed an eternity. Then it swung back a little.

From the binnacle the officer of the watch reported the ship's head steady.

Bracewell nodded. He shouted across to Kemp, 'She's held now. This is where we stay. God knows how long for.'

FIFTEEN

They were now totally at the weather's mercy. The ship lay right across the wind and sea that tore and smashed at its canted port side. Within a couple of minutes of her falling off in her heading, all the lifeboats along the port side had been smashed to splinters, the remains dangling from the davits for a while before being blown clean away. The *Orlando* lay in the trough, the trough from which there was no possible escape, pounded and hammered by the sea's weight. The shriek of the wind was now above them, passing over their heads from trough to trough, but the ship's motion as she wallowed and went on filling with water amidships was frightening.

By now, except for the ship's personnel required for duty and for the troops manning the pumps, there was no movement. Everyone remained where he or she had been when the Commodore's last warning had come, wedged, clinging on for their lives, more of them sustaining physical damage from shifting furniture or being torn from the grasp of tiring muscles. Sea-sodden, Miss Hardisty and a group of her girls were in a corner of the A deck lounge, more or less safe behind a big settee that had become wedged across between a pillar and the bulkhead, and didn't seem likely to shift again. Although scared to death, she was keeping up a brave face; as she had done before on other fraught occasions, she suggested singing.

One of the Wrens asked if she meant a hymn. She said that would be a good idea; she had always liked *For Those In Peril*

164

On The Sea and now she started singing it and they all joined in, the troops as well.

When the hymn ended, Miss Hardisty was crying unashamedly.

ii

OC Troops had been with the Captain and Commodore in the wheelhouse when they had been caught by the offswing and now he had to remain. He was clinging onto the sill where the glass of the port side-window had shattered under the sea's impact and he had been unable to let go for fear of being hurled across the wheelhouse. He was wet to the skin; they all were. As the ship steadied in its position of extreme danger, he spoke up.

'Is this sort of thing normal, Captain?'

'In a typhoon . . . yes and no.'

'An inconclusive answer.'

'That's the way things are, Brigadier. It's always possible to broach-to in a typhoon. As I said on the tannoy – when you have no engines, it's inevitable.'

'But surely good seamanship –'

'I'll thank you not to question my seamanship, Brigadier.'

'Well – no, I don't, of course. Perhaps some explanation might help, however.'

Bracewell looked across at Kemp, lifting an eyebrow. Kemp took the meaning: Bracewell, in a time of extremity, wasn't going to be bothered with OC Troops. Kemp took over and explained about typhoons at sea and the effect of being brought across the wind and sea, but Pumphrey-Hatton very clearly lost interest after a minute or so. He was concerned now about his comfort.

'Wet clothing,' he said. 'That can't go on. Too risky – we still have the cholera aboard.'

Kemp reminded him that the companion ladder from the chart room to the Master's deck was still available: he could go from there to his stateroom if he took care, and didn't venture onto the open deck.

'Yes, a good idea.' oc Troops, with Kemp's assistance, went gingerly across the wheelhouse and into the chart room. Bracewell watched him go, then met Kemp's eye.

'Not a word about his soldiers, Commodore. Or us, come to that! We're as wet as him.'

Kemp grinned. 'You could have put that a little better, Captain.' He went across to the fore screen. The glass ran with water, the spin of the Kent clear-view screens now stopped along with all other electric power. It was almost impossible to see anything, but there was in fact little to see apart from the huge waves on either beam, waves that ran on their courses beneath the ship to lift her bodily and then, as they passed, drop her down again into the next trough where she rolled soggily like a dead thing. The next time one of those waves went beneath him, Kemp opened the wheelhouse door and went out into the open wing. The wind hit with the force of the an express train, but he clung on to the teak rail and looked around, finding it hard to keep his eyes open when facing the wind. In the short time before the ship once again dropped and the wind and its deafening shriek was cut off, he was able to see the close horizons, the distance drastically cut by the appallingly close visibility. But he did see, or fancied he saw, something else: another vessel that he couldn't identify for sure. He waited for the next uplift to the heights, but this time saw nothing but those close horizons, the impenetrable walls of spray and flung spume, like a thick white carpet over the sea's turbulence.

He went back inside for a word with Bracewell.

'I couldn't be sure, Captain. The eyes play tricks in these conditions.'

'Yes, I know. Let's hope they did this time.' Another ship so close represented yet more danger. Any collision in such conditions would be fatal to all hands. All hands and the cook, as they used to say in the days of sail, as if the cook didn't count. Kemp went out again to the bridge wing, this time with Bracewell, and they watched, straining their eyes through the murk, trying to keep the binoculars focussed, a hard job in itself.

'There!' Kemp said suddenly, and indicated a bearing with his outstretched arm. 'See it?'

'Yes. Certainly a ship. Can you identify?'

'No. Now she's gone again.' They waited for the next upsurge and the one after that. Then again: and there was no doubt that they had another ship too close for comfort, a ship undergoing similar difficulties though most likely with her engines intact. Neither Kemp nor Bracewell could make a positive identification though both agreed she gave the appearance more of a warship than a merchant vessel.

'Not a battleship,' Kemp said. 'Could be one of the cruisers. Or a destroyer. I can't be sure . . . except that she's there.'

'What do you make the distance, Commodore?'

Kemp shrugged. 'Very hard to say. A guess – six cables.'

'Just about.' Six cables was 3,600 feet, say three-quarters of a mile.

'Nasty,' Bracewell said.

iii

Petty Officer Ramm, his role in charge of the guns now interrupted until better times came along, was helping out at the pumps, taking charge of squads of pongoes as they laboured and sweated, uttering words of encouragement as he had done to his guns' crews.

'Come on now, put some guts into it, a few pulled muscles and broken backs don't signify now, all right? You'll all 'ave 'eard of Davy Jones's locker I don't doubt.'

One of the privates looked up at him. 'What's that, a knocking shop?'

'Not the sort you'd like, lad. Knocking bones, maybe. Matlow's idea of 'ell.'

'Not what I heard, PO.'

'What did you hear, then?'

'Sailor's idea of hell: where all the bottles have holes in 'em and none of the women have.'

Ramm said sourly, 'Go on, get on with it, lad.' Women, with or without attributes, were a mixed blessing. The barmaid at the Golden Fleece had had plenty of attributes, as well as he knew, and he was still worried about her, dead worried about

167

the fact she'd let on, last time home in Pompey, that she knew his address, something he'd always been very, very astute about not letting her know – or thought he had. He was scared stiff . . . the missus must never get to know. Now he knew he was facing the possibility of early death; he didn't believe they were going to come through this and he wanted to make amends. There was no way, of course. He didn't believe for a moment that God would pay any attention to a plea from a sinner like himself, a plea that some divine intervention should keep the missus and the barmaid far apart – a difficult job in itself, since the Golden Fleece was less than a tram ride from his home. God would only say it served him right. As he uttered his routine chant of '*Hup*, down, *hup* down' at the toiling soldiers, Ramm's mind was absent. He might compose a letter to the missus, full of fibs of course, saying that he'd bought the barmaid the odd drink in the Golden Fleece and she'd taken advantage, or tried to, wanted to get him into bed and he had refused point-blank. But he knew the missus wouldn't ever believe that one. If only he could think up something foolproof that would scupper the barmaid in advance . . . but he couldn't. And anyway, how would the letter reach Pompey if the ship went down? Put it in a bottle? He told himself: don't be bloody daft!

After many more minutes of worry Ramm became aware that someone was watching him and looking sort of sardonic. Ex-Colour Sergeant Parkinson.

'What's that look supposed to mean, eh?' Ramm asked.

'You tell me, PO. Know what? You're out of step.'

'How d'you mean, out of step?'

Parkinson grinned. 'You're saying *hup* when the brown jobs are going down. And down when they're going *hup*.'

'Fuck off, can't you?'

Parkinson said, 'Your mind's not on the job. That's bad.'

'Got me worries, haven't I?'

'So we all have. Like, what's going to happen to the ship. What's yours in particular? Tell your sea-daddy.'

Ramm gave him a hard look: petty officers, unlike ordinary seamen, didn't have sea-daddies. But sea-daddy was about right as it happened – Parkinson was a real oldie for seagoing,

made even him look a youngster. Also, he'd been around –
Royal Marines first, then another lifetime in the liners, in the
passenger days when he must have seen plenty, especially as
a nightwatchman which was only another term for night
steward. Floating gin palaces, floating brothels. Parkinson
was a man of experience and had asked him the question. He
might have the answer. Ramm broke off from the pumps.

'Women,' he said.

'Ah?'

'Missus and –'

'The lady love. Well, well. You know what sailors are, as the
admiral said to the lady. Juxtaposition, eh?'

Ramm looked puzzled. 'Never 'eard of that position.'

'Never mind. I got the picture. More fool you, PO. Too close
to home – that it?'

'Yes.'

Parkinson poked him in the ribs. 'You should have kept it
buttoned-up,' he said, and moved away on the slant,
negotiating the heavily listed deck as the liner did one of her
slides down a watery mountain. Ramm cursed savagely and
went back to his job.

iv

The cholera had not left the ship; the seas and winds had not
washed or blown her clean while in her extremity. Dr
Crampton and the army medical teams were working round
the clock still, the various burns cases and other injuries
adding to their work-load. They were mostly out on their feet
but were carrying on. There were more deaths and more new
cases, though the rate was tending to drop. The latest to be
reported sick, not long after he had left the wheelhouse, was
OC Troops. His batman had gone to the medical section and
said the brigadier was vomiting. Colonel Munro himself went
at once to Pumphrey-Hatton's stateroom, where OC Troops
bitterly blamed the fly-blown gin.

'Dirty ship, Munro.'

'I doubt if it was that, sir. Too long past.'

'Oh, dammit, *more* fly-blown gin then!' One thing: the typhoon had finally disposed of the flies, blowing them to extinction. OC Troops said as much. 'The clean air of God.'

'I beg your pardon, sir?' Munro, busily taking samples for analysis, hadn't heard.

'The clean air of God!' OC Troops snapped, and was sick again. 'Blown the buggers to glory,' he said when the spasm had passed. Munro went below with his samples and confirmed the cholera. He remarked to his number two that the brigadier had appeared to be wandering already, a bad sign. He made a poorish report to the senior battalion commander, seeming to suggest a warning that Pumphrey-Hatton might not make it and that he had better stand by to take over. The lieutenant-colonel concerned thought fleetingly about early promotion, but knew that in any case it might not last long enough even to register at the War Office. But he knew what his duty was now, and he went at once to the brigadier's quarters to take any orders Pumphrey-Hatton might wish to give for execution whilst on the sick list.

'Just that, Colonel?'

'Sir?'

'Just while I'm sick, man! Or do you imagine I'm dying?'

'No, sir, not –'

'I expect,' Pumphrey-Hatton said disagreeably, 'you hope I am.'

v

Radar would have been useless now; the only echoes would be those that came off the waves. The unknown vessel had to be watched for by human agency alone, and that meant the bridge personnel – not long after Kemp had made his first sighting the foremast had been ripped out from the ship, breaking away from its heel like a beanpole and carrying the masthead lookout with it, as it smashed over the side to starboard and was almost immediately lost to view in the boiling sea. Kemp, remaining now in the bridge wing on constant watch, knew he was wasting his energy since there would be nothing anyone could do if the other ship and themselves were driven together. But those in authority had to be seen to be ready. To remain in the wheelhouse would not do. Troops, any more than civilian passengers, didn't know the sea. Aboard any ship there was one man and one man only who was strictly never off duty, and that man was the Captain. In a convoy at war stations, the same applied to the Commodore. And the enemy was still, or might be, in the vicinity.

Currently, however, it was the weather that was the main and very present enemy.

Captain Bracewell was sharing the vigil in the bridge wings, taking the port side for his watch. Kemp saw nothing but the sea itself, and no report came from Bracewell. It was dark now, dark not just from the lowering sky but from the encroaching night. Hanging in gimbals over the binnacle, the useless binnacle, was a storm lantern with a flickering candle, its light enhanced by mirrors. Kemp, glancing towards the water-drowned wheelhouse windows, saw something he didn't expect: the outline of a woman. He recognized Jean Forrest.

A moment later the starboard door opened and she came out into the screaming wind. Kemp shouted at her to get back inside, but the wind sent his words flying away. She was blown towards him like a leaf in a gale, and he caught her, wrapped his arms around her, held her fast as he leaned back against the angle of the teak rail.

'What the hell,' he said furiously. Her hair blew in the wind, all rat's-tails. She wore an oilskin about ten sizes too big for her. She was shivering. Kemp said, 'You've no damn right out here.'

'I know. I'm sorry.' He believed she was crying. 'I've been with OC Troops . . . doing what I could. He's wandering . . . I don't really think it's the cholera. I believe he's a bit unbalanced or – or something. He talked at random, a lot of creepy stuff about death and corruption and the inevitability of the grave. And there's been so much death.'

'I know that.' Kemp's tone was still brusque. 'It's a fact we have to accept.'

171

'Yes,' she said, 'I know, of course. But I . . . I don't think I can take any more. I'm scared. I – I wanted reassurance, I suppose. So I came to you.'

She was obviously crying now. Her voice had broken. Kemp held her tightly to his body. He said, 'Don't worry. We've come this far and we're not beaten. The worst the weather can do and we're still afloat. It'll moderate before much longer. Nothing goes on for ever, Jean. The worst of storms blow themselves out.'

He was scarcely conscious that he'd used her name, Jean. And a moment later it would have been forgotten in any case. A shout, faintly heard as it came on the wind from Bracewell, made Kemp look up sharply in time to see the shape dead ahead, the exposed side of the other ship lying right across the troopship's track as she wallowed in the deeps of a trough.

SIXTEEN

Nothing to be done – nothing, except watch and wait. Kemp's gloved fingers gripped the guardrail tight while his other arm remained for her safety around Jean Forrest. In the port wing Bracewell shut his eyes and waited for the impact. If the huge weight of the *Orlando* took the ship – she had switched on a searchlight and in its loom he believed he had recognized her as one of the destroyers of the escort – then she would be cut in two, a case of a knife through butter when the great stem struck thin steel sides.

It happened fast; but afterwards both Kemp and Bracewell felt they had seen it in slow motion. Their reports, their recollections, were similar: the destroyer, if such she was, had been deflected by a big wave, her head thrust to starboard, and then her whole hull was moved aside so that she crossed the *Orlando*'s bow, becoming for a moment invisible beneath the overhang, and then emerging with her searchlight blazing to crash her way down the troopship's port side, crushing her thin plates against the bulk of the big vessel. Quickly then she was gone, lost in the sea's violence, drifting further and further astern until her seachlight was lost in the flying spray and the general murk of the night.

'Inside,' Kemp said, and propelled Jean Forrest back into the wheelhouse. Bracewell came in through the door from the port wing. He said, 'That was a near thing, Commodore. That ship'll be in a bad way now.' He passed orders down for the chief officer: soundings had been taken continuously but now there was a need for the carpenter to make a thorough check right along the port side.

ii

The impact had been scarifying below. The bouncing of the destroyer off the plates had sounded like a series of giant-sized hammer blows, making the ship ring and clang throughout her length. Those in the lounges, still jam-packed, had seen the terrible sight for themselves as the loom of the searchlight had briefly entered by the big windows as the ship drew aft and away. A broadcast from the bridge gave them the facts, assured them that a check was being made. Miss Hardisty got down on her knees, clearing a space with some difficulty, and prayed as she had never prayed before. She believed her prayers had been answered when half-an-hour later the tannoy came alive again and Commodore Kemp spoke.

'There is no cause for alarm. The ship has not been damaged further. We are taking no more water than before. And it's extremely doubtful if any other ships are close, though I can't promise this.' There was a pause. 'I have good news for you. The wind is tending to decrease. By dawn I expect to be in calmer water. That is all.'

Miss Hardisty, her hands still clasped, said aloud, 'Oh, *thank* you, Commodore,' and then, recollecting herself, added, 'and God.'

iii

The reports to the bridge had been reassuring, enabling Kemp to make his broadcast. The army had done and was doing a good job and the ship was no lower in the water.

'So what's the prognosis?' Kemp asked Bracewell. 'What happens when we come out of the storm? Is it, in your view, going to mean abandoning?'

'Yes and no,' Bracewell said. 'We'll stay afloat – but we won't be getting anywhere.'

'A tow,' Kemp said. 'If the cruisers are still around. Or the *Valiant*. You think she'll stand a tow?'

'No reason why not. The damage is amidships. It's not as though we'd be pushing into the sea with a gaping bow. Let's leave it, Commodore. See what the dawn brings.' Bracewell added, 'We still have the wireless office as a going concern. We could ask Aden to send out tugs if there are no other ships around.'

'And risk the German? She may still be out there, you know, Bracewell. Probably is. I've an innate dislike of breaking wireless silence at sea.'

'But unless we do –'

'No. I still have the convoy to consider. God knows where they all are at this moment, but I can't take any chances of homing the *Admiral Richter* onto them. Aden'll realize.'

'Then what do you suggest?'

Kemp said wearily, 'I've already suggested the possibility of a tow, Bracewell. Now I'll follow your own suggestion: let's leave it till the morning. Then we can better judge the position, anyway if the wind continues to moderate.'

'It'll do that all right, it'll follow the usual pattern. We're through the worst of it.' Bracewell hesitated. 'If I may make yet another suggestion, Commodore, it's this: why not go below and get some sleep?'

'Oh, I'm all right. You're as whacked as I am anyway.'

'But it's my ship. And you're not all right, you're dead beat. I might point out that I'm a year or two or three younger than you. At our time of life, that counts. There'll be many decisions to be made in the morning. You'll need your sleep. As Commodore, I think *that*'s your duty.'

As the *Orlando* gave a sudden lurch to the still mountainous seas, Kemp reached out a hand to steady himself against the binnacle, and missed. He went flat on the deck of the wheelhouse, bumping his head on the binnacle support as he did so. He was helped to his feet by Bracewell, who said that he believed his point had been made.

Kemp went below. Bracewell would call him at once if he was needed. He found his cabin something of a shambles; in the emergency his steward had been needed elsewhere.

175

Drawers hung open, spilling their contents. The photographs on Kemp's desk had fallen to the deck, the glass was broken, the silver of the frames dented. That of Mary his wife was ruined, wet from a carafe of water that had sprung from its rack by the bunk.

Kemp went along himself to the Captain's pantry. The whisky bottle in his cabin beckoned, but this he eschewed. In the pantry he made himself a hot, strong cup of coffee. Having drunk this, he went back to his cabin. But he knew he wasn't going to find sleep and if he did by some chance then it would be a time of nightmare. His mind was still too active, too filled with past events and future decisions. No, he wouldn't sleep.

He reached for his uniform cap and put it on. He would make the rounds of the ship below decks, and talk to the men. It might bring some sort of comfort. To himself as well as them.

iv

Kemp found the packed lounges and other public rooms hard to penetrate. There was a certain amount of light from his own battery torch and others being used by the troops, occasional flickers that briefly lit the scene. A sergeant saw his gold-edged cap peak and got to his feet.

'Gangway there, gangway for the Commodore!'

'No ceremony, please, Sergeant. I'm not here to be a damn nuisance.'

'Sir!'

'What's it been like?'

'A fair degree of hell, sir, but nothing we can't take.'

'It won't be for much longer, Sergeant. We're coming out of it.'

'I see, sir. A good thing, sir, if I may say so. If I may ask a question of you, sir?'

'Of course, go ahead.'

'What's next, sir? What can I tell the lads? Some of them, they're worried sick.'

Kemp smiled. 'That's not surprising. They don't know the

sea. I do, so do all the ship's officers. Captain Bracewell and I were at sea in the old Cape Horners, smashing into the westerlies off the pitch of the Horn. That was real weather! It was hell, but we came through, and *we* hadn't any engines either. You can tell your men that we're coming through again, though at this moment I can't say just what comes next, whether or not it'll be a tow.'

'Very good, sir. I'll tell them that, sir, straight from the Commodore.'

Kemp moved on. There had been no point in telling that sergeant that not all the Cape Horners had come through. There had been many lost, many ferocious injuries and many deaths from falling aloft in the ships that did come through. Nor was there yet any point in saying that he, Kemp, was fast coming to the conclusion that they might have to abandon once the weather had moderated enough to get any un-damaged boats and rafts away. Abandon, and await rescue from Aden, where the naval HQ would know there had been a battle because, since once engaged there was no further point in maintaining wireless silence, the senior officer of the escort had transmitted the current position of the *Admiral Richter*. The subsequent silence from the Arabian Sea would not be hard to interpret and as soon as the weather permitted the rescue would be mounted.

That was the best hope now.

Kemp walked among the sick, having a word here and there when he saw a man awake and watching him. They seemed to appreciate it, and he was able to calm a few fears. The very fact that the Commodore had left the bridge to come below spoke for itself.

He met Jean Forrest in an alleyway as he was making his way back to his cabin. She seemed ill-at-ease. In a low voice she said, 'I want to apologize, Commodore. For coming to the bridge.'

'You're forgiven.'

'That's – very nice of you, Commodore.'

'Not at all. I understood very well.'

'It won't happen again, I promise.'

He nodded; he certainly wasn't going to encourage bridge

177

visits. But he said, somewhat self-consciously, 'When we get
to Trincomalee, and we *are* going to get there . . .'

'Yes, Commodore?'

He said, 'Oh . . . it's not important, Miss Forrest.' He
moved on, leaving her to stare after him. He'd been going to
suggest they might meet somewhere in an unofficial capacity;
he was relieved, really, that he hadn't. He went into his cabin
and took up the spoiled photograph of Mary, which before
going below he'd tried to dry off with a towel. He looked at it
for a long time. Yes, he was glad he'd turned matters off in
time.

v

The dawn came.

It was not a pleasant sky but the wind had all but gone and
the seas, though restless still with a heavy surge left behind by
the typhoon, were free of the pounding immensity of the
waves. The *Orlando* rode better now, no more heave and
lurch. Miss Hardisty in the main lounge came awake to find
light stealing through the windows. Close by one of her girls
snored loudly. Wren Peters – it would be. Miss Hardisty
poked at her with a finger.

'Stop it, girl, it's unseemly.'

'What?'

'You heard, Wren Peters. All these men.'

'Well, I like that! Anyone'd think I'd –'

'There's no call for impertinence.'

Wren Peters sulked and snuffled. Miss Hardisty produced a
handkerchief and ordered her to blow her nose. The WRNS
had to maintain its dignity, which the Lord knew was a hard
job in the present circumstances. After a while Miss Hardisty
climbed to her feet, smoothed down blouse and skirt, which
she'd now worn for far too long, a lifetime it felt like since
she'd last undressed, and made her way through the clutter of
waking soldiers, out to the promenade deck where she took a
walk up and down, and took a look at the sea.

She couldn't see any other ships. The German raider must

178

have gone, and praise the Lord for that. But where was the convoy? She was sure Commodore Kemp must be very worried about that.

Kemp, back now on the bridge, was, though he had hardly expected anything different. To Bracewell he echoed Miss Hardisty's unheard thought.

'Thank God the *Richter*'s not around.'

'No *Valiant* either. No escort. And I'm not thanking God for that!'

'Like the Ancient Mariner . . . all alone upon a sunless sea. Or whatever it was.' Kemp once again scanned the horizons all around the ship: nothing moved anywhere, a lonely scene. He said abruptly, 'Time for those decisions, Captain.'

Bracewell was about to answer when a voice-pipe whined in the wheelhouse. The Officer of the Watch bent to take the message, slammed back the cover and came out fast to report to the Captain.

'Carpenter, sir, reporting after sounding around. The level's increasing fast. Chief officer's on his way below.'

Bracewell swore. 'Does the carpenter know what's happening?'

'No, sir. He's flummoxed so far. He's –'

'He'd better unflummox fast at the double,' Bracewell said. He looked along the decks fore and aft, crowded with the troops who had come thankfully out from the lounges and other places of refuge now that the typhoon had passed. He looked down at the sea; there was that surge but on the whole the surface could be risked flat enough. Decisions were forming in his mind, but first he would await the chief officer's report.

That came after a quarter of an hour's impatient pacing of the bridge wing. The chief officer was as flummoxed as the carpenter. He gave it as his opinion that there was more damage from the *Admiral Richter*'s shell than had been suspected, and that something extra had occurred, some shift, as a result of the typhoon's pounding, something that had decided to shift only very recently.

'How much more water?' Bracewell asked.

'Increase of twelve inches in the last half-hour, sir.'

'Despite the pumps?'

'They're doing all they can, sir.'

'I'm starting to get the feel of the extra depth,' Bracewell said. 'More sluggish on the roll.' He passed a hand over the stubble of his cheeks; it was almost a gesture of resignation, of hope gone. He asked, 'What are the chances of making it good, a makeshift patching up?' Even as he asked the question, he knew the answer.

The chief officer said, 'None at all, sir. Just none. I believe there's a seam opening in the bottom plating, running right down through the double bottoms.'

Bracewell turned to Kemp. 'Too late for a tow even if there were ships around. This is it, Commodore.'

'You're going to abandon?'

'I am. It's all we can do now.'

'I'm with you,' Kemp said. 'Right away?'

'Right away. But no panic rush.' Bracewell went into the wheelhouse and took up the tannoy. Before he began speaking, passing the final order, Kemp said he was going down to see OC Troops.

vi

There had already been alarm: the word had spread when what had looked like a touch of panic had manifested itself in the ship's personnel. The chief officer had gone below at the rush, taking the ladders and companions at the double, his expression grim. The carpenter had been seen talking to the Staff Captain and two of the engineers with every sign of urgency. So the rumours started: they were about to go down. That had hastened the exit of the troops to the open decks, so that when Bracewell's voice passed the order to stand by to abandon ship they were mostly back already at their stations along the embarkation deck. Within a couple of minutes the ship's officers were in amongst them, doing their best to sort them out into new abandon ship stations, away from the smashed lifeboats on the port side. There were some ugly scenes as a number of the soldiers found themselves hustled towards the Carley floats, though in fact they were luckier

180

than those who would have to jump and hope for the best, hope to get a handhold on the lifelines rigged along the sides of the boats and floats once they were in. Miss Hardisty, a hen with her chicks, mustered as directed by the senior third officer at her original station on the starboard side.

She was assured that there would be no difficulty in getting the boats away. She asked, 'Do you know how long it'll be before we're picked up, Mr Wilbraham?'

'Shouldn't be long. The Captain's authorized a mayday call, and it'll be transmitted until the wireless room packs up.'

Miss Hardisty looked alarmed. 'Won't those Germans hear it?'

'Probably. But the Captain had no choice. It's better to be picked up by the Germans than just be left to float around.' The senior third officer moved away; he had much to do. Before he went he said the Germans would treat them decently. Miss Hardisty wasn't so sure about the Germans' merciful intentions, however, and she had no wish for her and her girls to spend the rest of the war in a POW camp in Germany. That Hitler, he was a brute and he issued brutal orders, and it was quite possible the *Admiral Richter* would open fire on the survivors rather than pick them out of the water, wasting time while the British Navy got on their track. She had heard that in fact they *had* fired on boatloads of survivors sometimes, and she had heard also that the German soldiers spitted French babies on their bayonets and roasted them over open fires, though she wasn't sure that hadn't been in the Great War.

Mustering his guns' crews at their stations, Petty Officer Ramm wasn't too worried about who picked him up, just so long as someone did. There were, he understood, sharks in the Arabian Sea, cruising up from the Indian Ocean.

Not very nice.

vii

'A matter of courtesy,' Pumphrey-Hatton mumbled from his sick bed.

181

'Which is why I'm here,' Kemp said. 'I –'

'Yes, yes, but I didn't mean that. I mean Bracewell should have had the courtesy to inform me *before* passing the order. I have the responsibility of my troops, damn it!'

'The order had to be given,' Kemp said heavily, 'and it had to be given without delay. I've come down to explain the situation –'

'Do so, then. First, be so good as to get me a glass of water, a *clean* glass.'

Suppressing anger, Kemp went to the bathroom and ran the tap. The water was turgid. He brought the glass to OC Troops, who drank. He didn't seem very bad to Kemp's non-medical eye. 'Now go on, Commodore.'

Kemp explained. Assistance, he said, would be on the way. OC Troops would be disembarked into a lifeboat with his staff. He could, if he wished, Kemp said tongue in cheek, carry on the military command from there. Pumphrey-Hatton interrupted to say, testily, that he believed Captain Bracewell to be panicking: the ship felt perfectly all right, perfectly steady, to him. Kemp didn't bother to argue; but before he could go on with his brief exposition the brigade major entered, accompanied by a staff sergeant and two of the ship's stewards, one of whom carried a Neil Robertson stretcher. In the rear was Colonel Munro. OC Troops would be in good hands. Kemp made thankfully for the door, heading for the bridge. As he left he heard sounds of argument, Pumphrey-Hatton's high-pitched voice protesting about something or other. Perhaps there had been fly-blows on the stretcher.

On the bridge, Bracewell was watching out for any ships and finding the seas still blank and empty. He and Kemp paced the wing. Bracewell took reports as they came in from the deck officers responsible for the muster along the embarkation deck and the safe lowering of the boats once they had embarked their loads. The bridge was awaiting the final report from the Staff Captain that all crew spaces and military accommodation had been cleared and all personnel on deck ready to go. It was understood between them without a word being said that Kemp and Bracewell would be the last to leave the ship. The tradition of the sea held. And, again, without it being mentioned, each knew the other had reservations about his personal survival. Captains, by tradition, had once gone down with their ships, Captain and ship being considered a single entity, one and indivisible. In Kemp's view, the same could be said of the Convoy Commodore. He dreaded being shipped back to the UK as a passenger, to report the apparent loss of a whole convoy as constituted after leaving the port of Alexandria.

He caught his assistant's eye. He believed young Finnegan understood what was going through his mind. He said abruptly, 'Finnegan, you have my home address.'

'Yes, sir.'

'If I don't come through, I want you to go and see my wife.'

'Sure I will, sir.' Finnegan hesitated. 'Are there any special messages, sir?'

'Oh, just say I did my best, Finnegan. We all did. That's all. And my love – of course.'

He was obviously embarrassed. Finnegan said, 'That's all right, sir. I'll do just what you want. But I guess it won't come to that. I guess we're going to get picked up. We're not all that far out from Aden.'

Kemp didn't answer. He was staring out to sea, staring at nothing, many things going through his mind. Bracewell too was silent now as the muster went on along the open decks, the shouts of officers and NCOS coming up to the bridge as though the troopship was a safe, shore-side parade ground with a brigade falling in for some sort of ceremonial. It all seemed like slow motion; but when the end came it came with terrifying suddenness. There was a curious noise from far below, a sort of growling as though from an angry giant caught in a trap of steel, and the ship lurched and seemed to shake herself, the stern going down, the bows lifting towards the sky.

SEVENTEEN

She lingered a little in her undignified position and a number of boats were got away in safety. The rafts were released by the seamen and shot down the slides into the water. Then three lifeboats, lowered hastily and clumsily, were upended before they took the sea, and their occupants spilled out, legs and arms flying. From the canted decks other men jumped, went deep, came up again to swim for the boats and rafts. Petty Officer Ramm was one of the jumpers and he was lucky: he swam for a lifeboat and was hauled aboard. In the boat he found PO Wren Hardisty. No sign of any other of the WRNS; and Miss Hardisty was crying.

Ramm more or less collapsed on the bottom boards. He wasn't as fit as he once was. He heard PO Wren Hardisty going on and on. He gathered she'd been manhandled into the lifeboat against her will by Nightwatchman Parkinson. She'd told him she wanted to stand by her girls, but he'd been quite brutal. He had said he would see to them after she was aboard, but there had since been no sign of Parkinson or the girls.

On the bridge Bracewell had hung onto the guardrail with Kemp and Finnegan, waiting for all hands to get clear. Yeoman of Signals Lambert had been ordered to leave and had obeyed with tears in his eyes. Finnegan refused point-blank to leave the Commodore's side. When the last moment came the three of them were still on the bridge. They watched as the stern slid further and the water rose from aft to the Master's deck, watched and steadied themselves as the canted bridge

184

came closer to the sea. There was a sound of tearing metal as the smokeless funnel was broken off by the force of the sea, and soon after this the water was lapping the bridge.

Kemp said, 'Time to go. No bloody silly heroics, Bracewell. You're more use as a ship's master than a dead hero.'

Bracewell didn't answer. His lips were moving silently; Kemp believed he hadn't heard a word. When the waters began to fill the bridge and wheelhouse, Kemp followed nature and struck out and away, he and Finnegan acting as one in laying hold of Bracewell and taking him with them. After all, there was now nothing left to stand by for. Useless tradition could be carried too far.

ii

From the boats and rafts they had watched the end, watched as the great ship slid away, shedding more and more men as she went lower. When she had gone there was a big sucking whirlpool and a number of swimmers were taken down by it into the depths. The sea was full of men, full of Neil Robertson stretchers carrying the worst of the cholera cases and being towed for the lifeboats by the medical orderlies and any others capable of assisting. Many of the swimmers, those cholera victims who were still in a weak state, never made it. One by one they vanished beneath the crowded surface.

Kemp had parted company from Bracewell and Finnegan. They had been torn apart soon after they'd started swimming, hit by the foretopmast yard as it had been dragged down onto them by the plunging motion of the ship. Kemp had been temporarily knocked out; he knew nothing of his immediate future, wasn't aware of being taken in tow by Nightwatchman Parkinson, late the Royal Marines, wasn't aware of being taken to a boat where hands reached down to heave his inert body aboard. When he did come to an awareness of his situation, he found Jean Forrest's arms around him.

They drifted, the overcrowded boats and rafts keeping together with scores of men clinging to the lifelines around each side. The Commodore's boat made its way around the fleet of small craft, Kemp using all his efforts to encourage the soldiers, giving them hope that rescue would come, getting singing started, something he half regretted when he heard the loudly sung words of some of the songs.

He caught Jean Forrest's eye and smiled at her. 'Pay no attention,' he said.

'Oh, I don't mind. It's not as important as keeping them going, is it?'

'No,' he said. 'It's certainly not. You too.'

'Me?'

'Keeping you going. But not too much. You should rest.' After all, she'd had the cholera and must still be weak to some extent quite apart from the current privations and uncertainties.

She said, 'Oh, no. I've got the Commodore to look after! That's quite a responsibility.'

He gave a grim laugh. 'Commodore of what?'

She said seriously, 'A very brave convoy that's had everything but the kitchen sink chucked at it. Don't denigrate yourself. You're being an inspiration now. You've still got a convoy, Commodore.'

He knew what she meant: the brigade major had gone round the survivors just as Kemp had done, and some sort of nominal roll had been called by the NCOs. A surprisingly large number of soldiers had come through: out of the whole brigade strength, around two hundred men had perished, not counting those already dead from the cholera, and sad though any casualties were, it could have been very much worse. The brigade would live on as such to help the fight against the Japanese forces in Burma. One of the survivors was Pumphrey-Hatton, who ordered his boat to be propelled towards the Commodore. He had a complaint to make: those suffering from the effects of cholera, of whom he was one, should have had cushions provided: the thwarts and bottom boards were hard. Kemp shrugged this off: all the cholera cases had their blankets and he saw that Pumphrey-Hatton also had his silk dressing-gown and that there was a flask in its pocket.

They floated, and for the rest of the day, when strength permitted, pulled under a blazing sun on a course to take them closer to Cape Gardafui and the approaches to Aden. As night fell they were growing more and more hungry and thirsty, the boats' rations being meagrely doled out; and there had been more deaths among the residue of cholera cases when just as the sun came up next day the ship's bosun reported smoke on the horizon. There was wild excitement; distress rockets were sent up and when the ship came closer Kemp saw that it was one of the armament carriers from the convoy, and that there was another behind her.

iv

Picked up to cram the decks and living spaces aboard the two big merchantmen, the troops gave three resounding cheers for the Commodore. Kemp acknowledged with a wave, but felt that Bracewell was the more deserving of recognition. Or would have been: Sub-Lieutenant Finnegan, like Kemp knocked out and subsequently picked up, had reported a lost contact, and Bracewell had not been seen again. Aboard the freighter to which Kemp was transferred he was given news. The *Admiral Richter*, finally hit by accurate and heavy fire from the *Valiant*, had settled with her main deck awash within minutes of the typhoon striking the convoy. She could not have survived it. *Valiant* and the cruisers of the escort were reported safe though damaged; two of the destroyers that had gone in with their torpedoes had been lost. The freighters were currently steaming for the rendezvous position. There, it was hoped they would re-establish contact with the escort and would then steam on in company for Trincomalee.

'Nice to have engines again,' Kemp remarked to Jean Forrest.

'We've been very lucky,' she said.

187

'I know.'

'And well led.'

'Rubbish! Don't flatter, Miss Forrest.'

'An order, Commodore?'

'Yes.'

She smiled somewhat enigmatically. They were sitting close together – they had to in the crowded conditions, far more crowded than ever it had been aboard the *Orlando*. Cabin accommodation would be organized somehow, the freighter captain had said, for the Commodore and the ladies, the latter being Jean Forrest and two of the Wren ratings who had after all been picked up along with most of the others. With the rest of the surviving girls, Miss Hardisty and oc Troops had been taken to the other ship, as had Petty Officer Ramm and Yeoman of Signals Lambert.

There were as yet many days before the Trincomalee arrival. Kemp was once again the Convoy Commodore, once again in a different ship. But when not required on the bridge he saw quite a lot of Jean Forrest: a night spent huddled together in an open boat had brought more than a touch of comradeship and familiarity.

At the rendezvous the last ship of the convoy turned up, together with the escort. All the rejoining ships, scattered by order of the Commodore and by the typhoon, had headed on westerly bearings before returning east. The cruisers had been steaming back for the last reported position of the *Orlando* as a result of the mayday call, but, finding only empty lifeboats and rafts, had headed for the rendezvous. Now all was well.

Something, after all, had been salvaged.

v

Trincomalee, in stifling heat and sunshine and with a reception committee. Once Kemp had withdrawn himself from the welcoming brass, he was driven in a staff car to naval HQ where he made his report, having worked on this whilst on passage from where they had been picked up.

The report rendered, he was allowed the peace of a room in

188

the naval quarters where he slept the clock round. When on his feet again, he was informed that he would be going back to the United Kingdom in four days' time, taking over a convoy leaving Colombo for Simonstown and thence the Clyde, a case of full circle. He was to leave almost immediately for Colombo on the other side of Ceylon. He didn't see Jean Forrest before leaving; but his allocated steward told him the lady had called while he was asleep. She wouldn't hear of his being disturbed. She, too, was under orders for Colombo. Not for passage home, but to take up an appointment at the Colombo naval base, and she had already left Trincomalee.

Kemp went by train to Colombo, a stifling and uncomfortable journey in a rattling carriage full of flies and heat and stale smells. It was not for a particularly personal reason that he made for the Gaulle Face Hotel; he had in any case been booked in there to await the convoy. But he knew that sooner or later all naval and military officers in Colombo would be found in the Gaulle Face. And when he went into the bar for a chota peg Jean Forrest was there.

She greeted him, getting to her feet as he approached. 'Good afternoon, Commodore,' she said.

He met her eyes. He said, 'My name's John.'

'Yes,' she said. She was a little embarrassed, he thought. He suggested gin and she said she'd like that. They talked and she said she, too, was staying for a day or two at the Gaulle Face.

'Then I'm in luck,' he said. 'We'll do some sight-seeing if you've time. I used to know Colombo . . . though a ship's master didn't get all that much time ashore. Except officially – the local dignitaries. I was taken to see the Temple of the Tooth at Kandy, for instance. And other places.'

'That would be nice – John. Thank you.'

They talked for a long time, of the convoy, of home, of other things. Kemp felt he hadn't been so relaxed for many months, for far too long. The war seemed right in the background, the bombs and shells, the torpedoes, the weather, the long slog across the seas, world without end. But now it seemed as though it had really ended, at any rate for a while. They had dinner together that night, a late dinner with drinks and

189

romantic surroundings. After dinner, coffee and liqueurs; all the comforts of civilization were at hand. They hesitated at the foot of the main staircase. Jean was looking a little distraite and was trembling. Kemp knew the signs. She murmured something about her room, then wouldn't meet his eye. He knew he was behaving rather like a schoolboy, not helping her out, leaving it all to her. The trouble was his mind was in a whirl, he didn't know what he really wanted deep down.

He took a grip. He said gently, 'Something you'd come to regret, Jean. Or I think you would.'

'Or you would, John.'

'Perhaps. I don't know. Ships that pass, Jean. Leave it at that?'

'If you want,' she said, and turned away. He watched her going up the stairs, rather fast. He believed she was crying. He went to the bar for another drink, a long one, and slow. Then he too went to his room. He took up the silver-framed photograph of Mary. He'd taken that to the *Orlando*'s bridge with him at the last. It was still smudged with the water from the carafe. He looked at it for a long time before he turned in.

Yes, he was glad he'd been firm. Quite glad . . .